Last Third

a novel

Jonathan Mach

North Loop Books | Minneapolis, MN

North Loop Books
322 First Avenue N, 5th floor
Minneapolis, MN 55401
612.455.2294
www.NorthLoopBooks.com

ISBN-13: 978-1-63505-120-9
LCCN: 2016902548
Distributed by Itasca Books

Lyrics on page 54 taken from Dave Reed and George Graff, Jr., "To the End of the
World with You," New York: M. Witmark & Sons, 1907.

Lyrics on page 59 taken from Richard Butler, John Ashton, and Timothy Butler,
"Torch," performed by Soft Cell on *The Twelve Inch Singles*, Polygram Records, 1999.

Lyrics on page 114 taken from Frank Sinatra, vocal performance of "Fly Me to the Moon,"
by Bart Howard, recorded with Count Basie and his Orchestra, Reprise Records, 1964.

Lyrics on page 140 taken from Walt Whitman, "A Noiseless Patient Spider," in
Leaves of Grass, 1891.

Lyrics on page 141 taken from John Donne, "No Man Is an Island," in *Devotions
upon Emergent Occasions,* 1624.

Cover Design by Rita Daniela Sere
Typeset by A.M. Wells

Printed in the United States of America

NORTHLOOP
BOOKS

Last Third

For Iris and John

PART I

CHAPTER 1

the end

PRESENT DAY.

The vintage aircraft made of metal tubes and aged fabric, its mahogany propeller slicing the salted sea air, flew past the last sliver of Fire Island on its way to the darkness of the Atlantic Ocean. Roy Higgins sat comfortably in the open cockpit of his Boeing-Stearman, a plane he bought sixty years before. His wedding photograph, framed in oak and shaped by his hands from the tree where they first kissed, lay in his lap.

Sarah Higgins was gone.

She was his compass, his companion, his life, lover, friend, and wife. Without Sarah, Roy wanted nothing of this world. She had been ravaged by Alzheimer's, the colorful memories of a shared life stripped from her one by one until she neither recognized her husband nor knew her own name. Life, as the wedding photo, was faded sepia.

He would not follow scripture or the words of Father Paul Joseph Flannery, the parish priest of Our Lady of the Snow, on their wedding day fifty years ago: "Unto death do you part." Death would not part them. Roy would follow.

"Aircraft squawking one-two-zero-zero, three-thousand feet, three miles south of Ocean Beach, state your intentions," the New York departure controller asked. Roy turned off the radio and the transponder.

The blip on the controller's radar disappeared.

"The future is yours, Jeremy, and so is she. Take care of her. To the defiant, to the rebels, and to the journey. You'll be fine. I promise. I promise! I'm going to be with my Sarah now," Roy said. He looked down toward the Atlantic Ocean. "We are all of the sea," he muttered.

No plane, however fast, can catch the setting sun. Through his arthritic hands the familiar rhythmic vibration of the Stearman's engine comforted him as he piloted toward his final end.

CHAPTER 2

code 0: unspecified

ONE YEAR EARLIER.

Three, two, one. At the end of every school day, like clockwork, Jeremy watched the red hand of the school clock trail toward due north and then bolted out the door of English class before the bell fell silent. It was a game that he played with himself. The type of game that only a single child could create, and laugh about, as if he had a make-believe friend to share in the laughter.

Jeremy was a loner who took refuge in himself. With no siblings and a father who had abandoned him long before he could remember, he trusted no one. Not even his mother, or so he thought.

At ninety pounds with chestnut brown skin, blue eyes, and untamed curly hair, he was the product of teenage parents. Children having children. Middle school was difficult enough, but being a mulatto bastard child made for challenging days in the rough and tumble world of middle school. Every time he looked in a mirror he saw a kaleidoscope of colors. Red, green, and blue or the combination of any two creating his mix of black, brown, and white skin color. Adults had names for everything, but none that he understood: mulatto, mestizo, biracial, multiracial, the list long. When he asked his mother about his "color," her answer had confused him as much as his reflection. "You're a product of the world, your ancestral past as vast as the globe. African, European, Caribbean, North American," Clare had said.

Choosing a race/ethnicity to fill out on the Scantron sheet of his eighth grade standardized test added to his confusion.

Code 3: Black or African, not of Hispanic Origin.

Code 4: Hispanic.

Code 5: White not of Hispanic origin.

Only allowed to choose one, Jeremy laughed, looking over at his classmate Haruto Suzuki.

"This is easy for you. Code 2: Asian," he said.

"No," Haruto said. "My mom says I'm not Asian, because it includes Chinese and I'm Japanese."

"You're sure you're not both?" Jeremy asked.

"Pure Japanese according to my mom. The Chinese are mules, a mix between horse and donkeys, she told me. And they eat dogs."

"What does that have to do with anything?"

"We have two dogs, and if I were Chinese they would have run away. Dogs know. They just know," Haruto said as he filled the circle marked Code 0 with his number two pencil. Jeremy followed. Code 0: Unspecified.

Jeremy knew where he stood among his peers. He didn't fit in, and in middle school there were only two camps, those who fit in and those who don't. Fitting in helps one survive, no different than the hyenas of the Serengeti or schools of dolphins in the oceans. Being shunned from the pack meant ridicule, chastisement, and the occasional scuffle with the lions of middle school. He couldn't swim with the dolphins nor run with the hyenas, and they reminded him why. The list was long: He had one parent and they had two. The color of their skin, their eyes, and their hair made "sense," they said. They had the latest iPhones, Nikes, houses (*not* apartments), pools, Xbox Ones, and clothes from American Eagle. And Jeremy did not.

There was a time when Jeremy wanted these things as much as the next kid. He asked his mother, but realized early in life the extent of her devotion was an occasional dinner of cold macaroni and cheese.

Clare Smith had given birth to Jeremy on Mother's Day. She watched as the doctor turned Jeremy on his side, trying to expel the amniotic fluid from the infant's lungs. To breathe and be human. To let go of the sea from which we all hail. "It was like J had no desire to be on this earth," she said. "The doctor had to cut me to get him, and the look on the nurses' faces. I thought he was stillborn. He never cried and I've never heard him cry. Ever. They'd never heard silence from a living baby before or after. But he did breathe . . . reluctantly and silently."

She never called him Jeremy, only J., insisting to all who asked that it was her father's name she bestowed upon her son, not her abandoned high school lover's. But Jeremy knew better. He knew little of his father but did know his name—Machado Jay Jackson. And when she called him J. instead of Jeremy, he wondered if it was out of pure laziness or a reminder of a love lost.

Clare, who had been popular with the boys and had excellent grades, had been the envy of both sexes. A committed student, she took advanced placement courses, volunteered at the local food bank, and was captain of the debate team and a member of the cheerleading squad. She accomplished everything she put her mind to and early in her senior year when the letter of acceptance arrived from Boston College, there were no prouder parents. The future was bright. But as is often the case, life is what you don't plan.

She became a teenage mother. Clare went from the most desired to the most despised. Falling from those heights was difficult enough, but she was unmoored by the scorn of those she held in highest esteem. She thought her parents loved her unconditionally, but that didn't include the baby. "Adoption is the best choice, sweetie," her mother said. "We're not talking abortion here."

The strains of school, pregnancy, and her parents became too much. Clare left school, gave birth to Jeremy, and eventually moved from her parents' house to one of the many nondescript basement apartments scattered throughout Long Island. She closed out her high school years when she found a large envelope buried among a stack of mail. Standing next to the mailbox, she opened it to see the golden seal of the State of New York stamped into the thick, coarse paper. And her name in large black script below the words "General Equivalency Diploma," both bleeding into each other from the falling rain.

Clare soon realized the difficulty of being a single parent. She never wavered in her responsibility to raise her son nor her love for him, but the toil of being the sole caregiver weighed heavy on her soul. The idealism of raising her son alone devolved into survival, then survival into subsistence living, which produced the only item she had in abundance—despair.

Children learn. They learn from their parents. They learn from their peers. Love, hate, bigotry, curse words, the list long and varied.

So what course would Jeremy set for himself? Would anyone ever wake him up to that place within himself that he would have to summon to take control of his life? Jeremy had the good sense to understand that life had more to offer, but he simply couldn't form the right questions. And then fourteen came and anger replaced silence. Fourteen will do that—biology, hormones, and nature are a stew not even the alchemist would dare to reckon with.

In his young life, Jeremy woke up and greeted the day with a "so" instead of a "yes." The rebelliousness of adolescence was pushing him to unknown places. Neither child nor adult, Jeremy was at the age of self-discovery. But what to do and where to go? His only instinct was to get away, away from life, people, himself. He had the worst of all traits.

He was neither enthused nor sad, he was . . . indifferent. To school, his future, his life. The kingdom didn't hold his interest. He didn't look to the world to ask why the moon was so gray or the grass so green. He had no interest in frogs, snakes, or the nature of anything, and when in a fleeting moment he asked himself why it was easier to pedal his bicycle up a hill in a lower gear, the thought left him as quickly as it was asked. But even a fourteen-year-old knows you can't get away from yourself or the world. He just had to look at his mother to understand that.

CHAPTER 3

the garden of eve

AT DAYBREAK, LIKE CLOCKWORK, Roy Higgins entered the South Shore Assisted Living Home carrying two coffees. He said polite hellos to the young ladies at the front desk, their attention split between the morning news on the TV and Roy's greeting. Roy signed in, taking great pride in his signature, always in proper cursive. It took longer to sign than in years past, but he abided by the rules taught to him in his middle school penmanship course a lifetime ago. He dotted the i's in "Higgins" and walked to Sarah's room.

He stood six feet two inches tall. In the spring of his life his boundless energy, generous smile, and interest in all that came before him made for a well-lived life. Now in his twilight, with gray hair and ageless hazel eyes, and captured in his weathered olive skin, he seemed undeterred by the slowing pace of his walk or his slight loss of mental ability. Roy had Sarah, and his kindly aged face and experienced manner was buoyed by his enduring love.

Roy refused to let the healthcare workers bathe or clothe her. He believed that it was his responsibility, though it was one of the many tasks provided by the nursing home. This was not home, this would never be home, but this was the hand that life had dealt.

Roy begrudged the name, South Shore Assisted Living Home, and the enormous cost of it all. It was part of the packaged plan, the five thousand dollars a month Alzheimer's Memory Care Plan to take care of his ailing wife, a plan the home required him to pay in full, but parts of which he forced them not to employ. A plan that would slowly bleed away their life savings.

Since the first day of their marriage, the ritual of making the bed, showering, and eating breakfast together was steadfast. Roy always made the coffee. Now the ritual included dressing Sarah and feeding her.

No sickness, however horrible, would stand between them. He knew that his life had changed the day she'd forgotten her birthday. Later she would forget his, and eventually her own name. It took a while, almost a decade, but as Sarah slowly faded into her own world, Roy's commitment and love were unwavering. He spoke to her as if they were still newlyweds, as if the blank stare would fade away and the loving memories of their life together would cure her illness. But deep down he told their story so as to not drown in the sorrows of his own grief. All things come to an end, but why must they end like this?

"Do you remember the first day we met, sweetie?" he asked, combing her hair as they both stared into the mirror.

With her golden blonde hair tightly finger curled and pressed against her porcelain skin, Roy had thought he'd seen an angel walking into civics class that first day of his senior year of high school. Only in the pages of Life magazine had he seen a woman with curves as beautiful as any architecture built by the hands of man. He observed, as did every lusting boy and envious girl, her svelte waist, determined shoulders, and nail polish that matched her coral-painted lips. Never before had he looked at a woman so closely and been moved so quickly.

"What are you looking at?" she asked with malice as she sat next to him. Speechless, he looked away, hoping the bright sun shining through the classroom window would mask his ruby-red blushing cheeks.

As the class's focus reluctantly turned toward their teacher at the front of the room, Roy sneaked another look at her. The country boy from Long Island didn't have an ounce of religion in him, but when he saw her two-inch heels and beautifully manicured toenails, he murmured, "God help me! Heaven be damned! Gus, what brings a girl like that . . . here?"

"Heaven be righteous, not damned," Gus replied.

Roy had met his best friend one day after Sunday mass. Roy had little use for church but attended out of respect for his mom. He did, however, refuse to attend religious education classes at the parish during the week. "One hour on Sunday is more than enough," he politely declared to his mom, with his dad in full agreement. Farm chores, his dad felt, would give Roy religion, and the two wholeheartedly agreed about that too.

Gustava "Gus" Gunther was a skinny, gangly kid with freckles and male-pattern baldness at the ripe age of seventeen. Altar Boy Gus, as his classmates called him, looked like something out of the fifth century BC, dressed in full clerical garb with sandals included. He was an easy target for the local bullies and, as luck would have it, or as Gus would say, "divine intervention," Roy was riding by on his bicycle as Gus was getting the religion beat out of him. Even with God on his side, Roy could see that Gus didn't have a chance.

Roy was a tall, lean kid who developed his muscular physique and tough mental attitude by working on his family farm. He wasn't adverse to fighting a bucking horse or going elbows deep into a cow's uterus to deliver a breeched calf. Mixing it up with a couple of rednecks, that was easy stuff. Saved from the bullies, Roy and Gus became lifelong friends.

"What if she's not Catholic?" Gus asked.

"Whatever she is, that's what I am," Roy said.

"That's blasphemy!"

"Amen brother, amen."

"I hear ya, nothing a little holy water couldn't cure."

Roy knew he wanted to be more than just next to her. To make her his wife, "and the two would become one flesh." She would become his religion.

Sarah's Hollywood look that first day of class would soon be traded in for the harsh reality of country living of which she and her mother were now part. Her father, a successful Wall Street man, had survived the Crash of '29 but not the Great Depression and long economic decline that followed. All that remained by the late '30s was the summer cottage on Long Island. He was, as Sarah said, the last casualty of Black Sunday. "One more year and Dad would have been all right. The war came one year too late."

Her father promised his family that they'd start anew. They'd farm on the small plot of land surrounding the cottage, eat fresh-picked sweet corn, and dig up cherrystone clams from the wet sands of the Great South Bay. But the despair and shame were too much for him, and he never made it to the island. After kissing his wife Eve and Sarah a last "good night," he retired to the English basement of their brownstone apartment on the Upper East Side of Manhattan. The muffled sound of a single shot awoke them both, and her mom's scream was forever etched in Sarah's memory. The strife of one life ended with an act as destructive to the living as the dead.

The obit page of the *New York Times* stated Albert Edward Wallace died in his sleep of natural causes, a white lie owed to the last vestige of influence his Wall Street friends still had.

Within days of his death they were evicted from their home. Sarah had little time to grieve, and when she did, she did not know whether she was grieving for her mom, her dad, or herself. She would never forget the last line of her father's obituary: "Survived by his wife, Eve, and daughter, Sarah." Survive? Is that all we do?

Just survive until our eventual end?

Sarah and Eve were ill equipped for the hardships of country life. The fresh-picked corn once served on gold-lined platters now had to be planted and harvested. Wood needed to be cut, split, and stacked to fuel the furnace and oven, and water pulled by bucket from the deep well for drinking and cooking. Chickens were fed, clothes washed, meals prepared, and a host of other responsibilities once done by servants now a distant memory. But even this was not enough.

Survival relied on the goodwill of the country folk who helped them through the lean first few years. Eve got part-time work at the local drugstore and Sarah gave piano lessons for a few dollars at the VFW. Seeing an opportunity, Roy wasted no time teaching a reluctant city girl how to live off the land. He showed her how to hunt pheasant, deer, wild turkeys, and rabbits and the proper way to hold a rifle and swing an ax. The correct seeds to sow—spring was for peas, radishes, greens, and onions. In the summer, potatoes, beans, squash, and pumpkin.

And she taught him of a sustenance of another kind. The poetry of Shakespeare, the simple majesty of Chopin's Nocturnes, the stark penned imagery of Tennessee Williams, the bebop jazz of Dizzy Gillespie. Roy had no taste for the opera nor Sarah for firearms, but all else the world had to offer was theirs to share, learn, and enjoy . . . together.

In her second year on the island, she fell in love with the country boy. A troupe of garter snakes made their home in a red maple tree next to the garden. While picking the bounty of a hard-earned summer crop, Eve ran into a few and screamed such a fright, a scream Sarah recalled hearing only once before, the day her mom discovered her dad dead in the basement. Sarah ran to Roy's house begging him to save her mother. Through his laughter he tried to convince her of the benefits of snakes, but Sarah would have none of it. Reluctantly he built a small fire beneath the red maple tree, smoked them out, and whacked half a dozen dead with his shovel.

With the snakes gone, the garden could no longer provide the bounty that it had. Insects and rodents took over until Sarah and Eve, realizing the error of their ways, asked Roy to find a few snakes and reintroduce them to the garden.

But it was on that day among the smoldering embers and dead snakes Sarah pronounced her undying love for Roy and revealed her family story. And as Roy told a thousand times thereafter, the story of their love and life together that began in the garden of Eve.

CHAPTER 4

bike speed

JEREMY RODE HIS BICYCLE everywhere—especially to school, as the lions of middle school didn't wait until he was on campus to ridicule and bully. He was fair game and it started on the school bus, a place he avoided at all cost. Even on those bitterly cold winter days Jeremy figured it was easier to bike to school wearing three layers of clothes than endure the scorn, slaps, and spittle.

Jeremy enjoyed the freedom of riding. The street, the sidewalk, the highway, the service road, the dirt road, the pavement, the back way, front way, short way, long way. All choices his to make; he was in control. Bike speed, as he called it, was his favorite gear. The heavy pull and burn on his young legs as he worked his way to the top of a hill, the bike an extension of his body. The pain and exhaustion, the exhilaration, all his and his alone. And then the fruits of his labor: the earned reward of gravity at the top, his bicycle shuddering not to break apart as it and the boy sped downhill. This exhilaration cost him a few bloodied knees and elbows. But these blows were on his terms, bestowed by the bicycle gods and not by the hands of bullies. Scars worn with pride. He counted nine different ways to get to school, but it was the tenth where this story began.

Every day the 7:10 local of the Long Island Rail Road passed south of James Wilson Middle School, carrying commuters to the heart of New York City. Within earshot of the school, its diesel locomotive blew its trumpet as it passed the grade crossing.

On this day, as he had done many a day, Jeremy inhaled the familiar spent trail of diesel exhaust as he pedaled furiously in an attempt to keep up with the accelerating locomotive. It was another game he played alone, another game only a single child could create. *I'll take that train one day and go to the ends of the earth!* he would laugh to himself, a whimsically insincere boast in acknowledgment of his own futility. Other than the one school trip to the Museum of Natural History in New York City, he'd never left Long Island. Anything beyond its shores might well have been on the other side of the world.

So for now it would be the short ride to school, and on this day the gravel road adjacent to the tracks would be the path to get him there. In the world of bicycle physics, bike speed and gravel don't mix. Jeremy knew that his bike would slow down as it raced from the dirt to the mixed gravel. It did, but not as the D-student had calculated. The front wheel dug in and the back wheel lifted and catapulted both bike and boy into the air. Time slowed, and like many of the fitful dreams that awoke him in the middle of the night—dreams not of flying but falling—Jeremy giggled, spread his arms, and flew as if he were in some comic book. The absurdity of it evoked the meaty laughter only a child can muster. He laughed as he fell in a puff of dust onto the sharp gravel.

His Trek bicycle bought for him by his grandparents and given as a gift by his mother had the last laugh. Discontent with gravel and bike speed, it came crashing down on his head. Both bike and owner lay splayed on the dusty gravel as the last few carriages of the westbound train to New York City passed, its passengers looking on in amusement and laughter.

The bike useless, Jeremy limping, and school now in question, he pondered what to do. He'd given his mother his word. He'd go as promised, bloodied and limping. He shouldered the bike and hobbled toward school.

He knew of a shortcut through the trails of the Sans Souci County Park. Considering his condition and that of the broken bike, it was the quickest way to go. And so he did, hiking the trail through oak and hickory trees.

As the light of day gave way to the dappled gloom of the forest, Jeremy wondered why people hike. *This isn't the Forbidden Forest of those Harry bullshit Potter novels*, he told himself, but he knew that he'd run as fast as his bloodied legs permitted if he were to see three-headed dogs, unicorns, or talking trees.

He scorned the nerds in school who spoke in fake British accents and carried the novels around as if some magical power were bestowed upon them after three hundred pages of fantasy. Jeremy understood unreality and its appeal, but he lived in the harsh reality of an indifferent mom, no father, and peers willing to impose the brutal dictates of humiliation. Dicks, all of them.

Deep into the park, the waist-high thickets of dense pepperbush and honeysuckle shrubs made for slow going. Civilization was an earshot away, but he couldn't figure in which direction. He could hear the sounds of cars traveling on Sunrise Highway, their echoes ricocheting off the wide tree trunks. Squeezing tighter against his body, he felt nature consuming him like a bug being eaten by a praying mantis, the green maze of thick brush and canopy limiting his view to a few feet.

"Maybe this *is* the Forbidden Forest!" he said out loud. "Are there vampires out here?" Fear was overheating his brain and getting the better of him. With all the strength his rising panic could muster, Jeremy turned away from the path and pushed into the dense underbrush toward what he believed was a distant light. "An opening in the forest!" he yelled.

Jeremy pushed toward the opening, each step forward through the brush as difficult as any hill he'd climbed on his bike. Suddenly his firm footing disappeared, and he sank chest deep into a hidden marsh of cold, muddy water. Every muscle in his body tightened, expelling the air from his lungs. Arms flailing and feet thrashing, his fear had turned to outright panic. He couldn't plant his feet nor turn toward solid ground. Branches and rotting vines snapped as quickly as he could grab them. He was drowning and he knew it. Now unable to keep his mouth above the swamp water, Jeremy couldn't breathe nor scream.

One last reach, one last try. Something. Anything! Then he felt a coarse, woody branch on the outside of his hand and quickly pulled it into his palm. It was loosely wrapped in a vine. With one final pull he rose from beneath the muck. The branch snapped but the vine held. He could breathe. He could see.

Snap!

The vine gave way and Jeremy fell back into the marsh, drawing his last breath, the light of day choked out by the water. *I am dying.* With that thought, a tranquil peace rushed over him, a peace that he had never experienced before. *It's true. Dying is easy, it's living that's hard.* "Take me now!" his hypoxic brain screamed, his mouth silent beneath the muck. And then another branch. He made a choice. Instinctual, but a choice. Jeremy grabbed the branch and pulled. He pulled with all his will, because life demands 'yes' instead of 'so' in order to live. It held and Jeremy muscled his way from the depths of the swamp onto the firm footing of the mossy ridge. He stood and looked back. "What a rush!" he screamed, still shaken by the experience, but adolescence doesn't permit much reflection. Perhaps next time.

Peering above the swamp water like the nose of an alligator was the bent rear tire of his Trek bicycle. His backpack was gone. "Damn it!

Damn it! Damn it!" he screamed, the salamanders and toads looking on at their uninvited guest.

Pop! Pop! Pop!

Gunshots! Jeremy dropped to his knees. Suddenly the forest came alive. The silence was now a lioness roar, even the thick oak and hickory trees bending to the will of the ferocious wind. It was as if the earth became unhinged. *My God, the Potterheads are right!* Battered by missiles of acorns, pinecones, and branches, he dug his fingers into the soft moss, but a wall of wind threw Jeremy back into the marsh. Grabbing a thick vine, the only lifeline between him and the belly of the marsh, he screamed, "Mom, help me!" This surprised him. *But who else is there? Who else is there?* The vine was slipping from his hand as the overpowering wind pushed him back into the throat of the hungry swamp.

Again he swallowed a mouthful of swamp water. It tasted of fungus, vinegar, and bitter mud. He wondered how he would taste to swamp rats and other creatures as he clung to the last inch of vine.

Then it stopped.

As quickly as it had begun, the ferocity of the wind subsided into a gentle breeze. "My God, she heard me!" A mother's plea to the gods for her son's life, he believed. Jeremy had never given much thought to a God or religion—the closest he'd gotten to a church was the sidewalk, speeding by on his bicycle.

He pulled himself out of the marshy swamp thinking of God and his mother. Covered in mud and foliage and smelling pungent, he trudged slowly toward the light. The forest of marsh and swamp gave way to a grass field and, to Jeremy's disbelief, a farm. *What the fu—*

An old man with a weathered face and gray hair stood there as if some prophet from the hereafter. Oblivious to his smelly intruder, he held what appeared to Jeremy as a metal wand. Next to him were an airplane and jeep as old as the man himself. *What the fu—*

"All right, Gus, one more time!" Roy yelled.

The top of Gus's bald head poked from the open canopy like a mouse from its hole. "Roger, prop clear!" Gus said. Jeremy watched as the discontent engine groaned from its sleepy state and awoke with loud pops of protest, spitting gray smoke smelling of oil and gasoline. The exposed engine shook the ground and stripped the forest bare of everything in the path of its powerful wake.

Jeremy read the word STEARMAN, letters written in black script on the yellow tail of the airplane, and the word jack next to the small rear wheel. *Jack Stearman—that old goat almost killed me!* Jeremy looked at the airplane with its yellow wings adorned with the capital letters US Navy, and realized this man and this machine the cause of his second near-death experience in less than thirty minutes.

The engine smoothed from a coughing sputter to a perfect purr, and both men grinned joyfully and saluted each other. "Take her back to the barn," Roy said. And like some elephant lumbering back to its watering hole, the powerful beast was taxied across the expansive grass field toward the old farmhouse on the far side of the farm by Gus.

"Hey, you! You! Jackass, or is it Jack Stearman?" Jeremy shouted.

"What the hell!" A wide-eyed Roy stepped back, raising his Sears Craftsman wrench as a weapon. Covered in mud and leaves and smelling of skunk weed, Jeremy barely looked human. He wiped his face with his muddy arm.

"What the hell you thinking, Stearman! You almost killed me!"

Roy looked at Jeremy, the woods from where he came, and back at Jeremy. "Who . . . what the hell are you?"

"What the hell am I? I'm trying to get to fuckin' school!"

A kid? Roy asked himself in disbelief. He looked closer. "My God! What the hell were you doing rolling around in the swamp?"

"I lost my bike and backpack in the goddamn swamp 'cause of you. You turned on that stupid machine and it goddamn near killed me."

"Where did you learn language like that?" Roy demanded.

"Cable TV, you old fart!"

"Why would you ride your bike into the swamp? You on drugs?"

"No! I just want to go to school! You deaf, old man?"

"I hear fine! And don't call me old man."

"You look old to me!"

"I may be old but I'm smart enough not to end up in the San Souci Swamp! What the hell they teaching you in that school? It ain't common sense!"

"I got common sense . . . geezer!"

"Common sense says to stay on the trail, you dumb ass!"

"You're a dumb ass!" Jeremy spat.

"You're a bozo!" Roy roared.

"Dickhead!"

"Nudnuck!"

"You're a queer!"

"That's it, skuzzball," Roy hissed, raising his wrench again. "I'm going to knock you on your ass!"

Self-preservation and common sense go hand in hand, and Jeremy skipped away from the angry septuagenarian. What he hadn't planned on was tripping over the tow bar connected to the vintage Army green Willys-Overland Jeep.

"No one calls me queer and gets away with it!" Roy said, standing over Jeremy and brandishing his wrench. "I'll knock some sense into you, you little shit. It might make you smarter, because you can't get any dumber."

"You can't hit a kid. It's illegal!" Jeremy pleaded.

Not the law but a timely landing of a Piper Cub just a few yards away saved Jeremy. Roy's eyes focused skyward for just for a moment. It's what all pilots do when they see a plane, and as he had done countless times since the age of six, during the barnstorming days, when a Curtiss JN-4 Jenny biplane had landed on the very field where he now stood. That day long ago, when the strange-looking machine flew barely above the tree line, its pilot waving, then signaling his intention to land, and Roy Sr. trying to wave the plane away, knowing he'd want fuel, shelter, or food for the price of a ride.

When Roy's mom saw her son wide-eyed in disbelief, with his mouth half open in amazement, she beckoned the pilot to land. She wanted a ride as well and was as thrilled as her son. Little Roy would sit on his mom's lap. She had read of the Wright Brothers, the daring feats of the barnstorming men of the day and later, the most famous of them all, the tall lanky kid they called Slim, he too also raised on a farm, on the banks of the Mississippi river near Little Falls, Minnesota, the one known as Charles Lindbergh.

This was the first time anyone in the family had seen an airplane. Roy Sr. resisted what he considered a frivolous exchange of hard-earned gasoline and food for what essentially was a hay ride around the farm. His wife couldn't argue the logic of his dissent, but logic didn't rule the day—she did. She threatened that Roy Sr. would never see the likes of her blueberry pie if he didn't change his mind. He did, and quickly.

"It was as if God himself had come down from the heavens and bestowed upon me the direction my life would take," Roy Jr. would later say. And on that glorious Sunday long ago, with the sun setting and the trees casting long shadows on their farm, Roy's mom bartered a few gallons of gas and a home-cooked meal of sweet corn, bacon-wrapped duck, and blueberry pie for a thirty-minute ride around the pasture.

"Betty," Roy said as the Piper Cub eased onto the grass to a gentle landing. This was the distraction Jeremy had needed to escape. By the time Roy turned his attention back toward Jeremy, the boy was long gone. Roy looked around wondering if his encounter with the wild "kid" from the swamp had been a figment of his imagination, if he too was losing his mind.

He walked toward the pressed grass, bent down, and ran his hand through it. He raised his hand to his face and smelled the muddied grass, vinegar, and rotting cabbage. He hadn't imagined. It was real.

CHAPTER 5

dirt and muck

JEREMY MADE HIS WAY into the bathroom trailing mud and swamp water. He jumped into the stand-up shower. The last remnants of dirt and muck grudgingly disappeared into the shower drain, but the day's events stayed with him. He could not fully grasp what had happened, but he knew he had lived through something. What that something was, he couldn't fathom. He could describe it—the bicycle, the swamp, the plane, and the crazy man. But it was more than just the events—a feeling stayed with him that he couldn't express, and all this before nine in the morning.

He had cuts and bruises all over his body: bloodied knees from the thick brush, and his palms were raw from the coarse vines that he had clung to for his life. He could have been angry. He wasn't.

He chuckled with the self-confidence of a young boy well-versed in the harsh ways of the world. His bike, backpack, and clothes destroyed, Jeremy laughed as the Buddha laughs, his stomach aching and his eyes tearing with mirth. *I survived another day—or at least the first part of this one.*

He finished his shower and cleaned the basement apartment of any evidence that he had dragged in. He had survived the morning's adventure, but his clothes had not. He threw his ripped jeans and torn, soiled shirt into a commercial garbage dumpster a few blocks from the apartment and settled in for the day. His mother would eventually find out that he was down to one pair of jeans, but that would be a battle for another day.

Afternoon television was a luxury foreign to him, but one his mother knew well. It was the first Wednesday of the month, so Jeremy knew that his mother was at the New York State Unemployment Office, trying to convince her employment counselor that she'd been looking for work. He'd gone with her since he was in a stroller and as he grew older watched as she lied about the list of businesses she'd purportedly contacted in search of employment, the list generated from the telephone book a few hours before and from the comfort of her couch watching daytime television. It was not only the lying, but the ease in which she lied that disturbed Jeremy. He couldn't stand going with her, and at fourteen he'd had enough.

"You lied to that woman. You haven't looked for work in months," he said.

"We need to eat and you need to mind your own business."

"And what business is that? Give it a name so you can lie about it next month."

The slap caught Jeremy by surprise. Her anger and embarrassment, her life and its shortcomings summed up in a smack. She had smacked him before, but this time it was different. She had hit him across the face. She had crossed a line and she knew it. The guilt was immediate, the regret instant, the consequences permanent. Jeremy fought back the tears as onlookers outside the unemployment office stared in disbelief or amusement.

"Look at me!" he demanded. She refused. "Look at me!" he screamed. She relented. He stared at her in cold silence as the side of his face and eye swelled. He wanted her to know who the adult was now. The embarrassment was all hers too, and no words could justify her actions.

The older he'd gotten the more distant they became, the slap cutting through their old relationship like a sword. Jeremy was convinced that from that moment on, she would learn something from him. It would take almost a month before he uttered another word to her.

Jeremy surfed the TV, his mind too disinterested to stay on one channel for more than a few minutes. He searched for nothing in particular, and daytime television had little to offer. He had enough drama in his own life to be interested in watching any of the daytime soaps. The people were too beautiful, their houses too big, their fridges too filled with food to be believable. The local news was death and destruction, a taste of which he'd experienced earlier in the morning. When Oprah appeared, a woman his mother quoted daily from things spiritual to material, from free cars to a personal makeover—none of which he knew Clare would receive—he shut the damn thing off.

Jeremy laid his head against the worn sofa pillows, closing his eyes and listening to the ensemble of discordant sounds bleeding through the door of the basement apartment. People talking, cars moving, little kids laughing, lawnmowers roaring, trucks braking. One sound mixed in with the others, familiar to him as the rest and there from the very beginning. He was taking notice for the first time.

Jeremy heard the distant sound of an airplane. He walked to the basement wall and looked up where wall met ceiling. There, through the grime and dirt clinging to the small basement apartment window, was a framed sliver of sky. Against the aqua blue sky he saw a tiny silver speck with a long white tail. For a fleeting second he thought of Stearman and laughed.

It's like the 7:10 train going to the city. I wonder where that plane's going? I'll take that plane and go to the ends of the earth one day. Delusions of youth perhaps, but what would youth be without it?

Jeremy walked back to the couch and turned on the television hoping, at least for a little while, that its hollow drool would distract him from the world in which he lived.

CHAPTER 6

home

THE BLADES OF CUT GRASS swirled out from behind the tractor like that of a boat's wake, their fragrance perfuming the crisp morning air. All who draw a deep breath of the sweet scent of morning dew and cut grass know they are among the living. Roy sat atop the red American Harvester as he'd done a thousand times before and remembered his first ride on his father's lap. By the ripe age of nine he was cutting the two hundred acres of fescue grass and had coaxed that very same tractor into cutting the same stretch of lawn till the present day.

Roy wasn't one to reminisce, but lately his mind had been forcing him back to his childhood. He wondered why, and with some reflection found his answer. Nothing lasts forever except the earth and sky: something he had always known, but this was not the denouement he'd imagined. By thought's end he would start crying. No one bore witness, but it didn't lessen the embarrassment and, like many men of his generation, he thought it unbecoming.

Roy knew the land because he was the land. Born and raised on this farm, which his great-grandparents had homesteaded a hundred and fifty years before, his only time away was three years during

WWII as a combat pilot in the Pacific. He would never leave again, nor did he want to.

The war had given Roy the gift of flight. Raised next to the sea and drawn to it, Roy often wondered why his dreams took place not by the sea but above it. But when the war broke out, naval aviation was an easy choice. The U.S. Navy taught Roy, along with tens of thousands of men (and a few hundred women), how to fly. Those who survived returned home with a skill they only read about or dreamed of as children.

To his surprise, he convinced his father. A farmer who lived frugally, as most farmers do, Roy and his dad went halves on a surplus Boeing-Stearman, the plane he'd learned to fly while in the service. Thousands were being sold by the government for pennies on the dollar. One hundred dollars was two month's labor, but Roy Sr. knew that was a small price to pay to keep his son on the farm. The lure of aviation beckoned his son from that first flight as a baby in his mother's lap. Roy Sr. listened politely to his son's insistence that the plane would be as useful as the tractor. "Son," he responded after a cynical laugh, "this farm doesn't exist without my American Harvester, and if you hit one of my Holsteins landing that contraption you'll be the worse for wear. Won't that be the shit! The Japs couldn't kill ya but a dairy cow did."

In his youthful enthusiasm, Roy had believed that crop dusting and hauling goods to the far ends of the island would bring a quick return on their investment. For Roy Sr., all that mattered was family and farm. His only child had survived the war, married Sarah, and, with a plane to keep him contented, would continue to work and live here as his grandfather and great-grandfather had done before him.

At first it was a working farm of Holstein and Guernsey dairy cows that produced milk, butter, yogurt, and cream. Eventually the large factory farms made the small family-owned dairy farms unprofitable.

Like the plow and shovel, thrift and ingenuity are equally important to the farmer. In time the cows gave way to a small sawmill. After the war, wood was in great demand and the maple, sweet birch, and oaks of Long Island brought needed income to the family. The tall oaks were felled with axe and muscle, the stumps pulled like a bad tooth with the American Harvester. Every bump Roy felt on the tractor was the story of a fallen tree and a time and place in his long life.

Eventually the land itself became more valuable than anything grown from its soil. Returning soldiers from the war, newly married and starting families, created a need for single-family homes. The postwar boom led to large swaths of farm and forest being bulldozed to make room for mass-produced suburbia. Levittown had arrived. The agrarian lifestyles familiar to Long Island that began with the American Indian and eventually led to the Dutch, English, and other European settlers were being lost to the ravages of concrete and asphalt.

Automobiles, fast food restaurants, and strip malls soon crowded in on the magnificent flocks of migratory waterfowl, hawks, and other wildlife that had defined the natural beauty of the island. Roy had long forgotten the last time he'd seen so much as a deer. What he had not forgotten was the day when a portion of the Hempstead Plains, thousands of acres of grassland from which Lindbergh had taken off on his transcontinental flight to Le Bourge, France, was paved in the "spirit of modernization" . . . into one of the largest indoor shopping centers of its time.

Difficult economic times forced Roy Sr. to sell a portion of the farm. He would be the first and only one in the long line of Higgins men to sell the land his great-great-grandparents had settled during the waning days of the Civil War. It secured them financially, but it was a sacrifice that Roy Sr. struggled with for the rest of his life.

The Levittown sprawl came in a uniform bloc: Caucasian. Roy Sr. may have been a simple family farmer with little education or travels beyond the limits of the island, but fairness and justice are not the sole domain of the well educated or well traveled. He also wasn't blind. The "restrictive covenant" ensuring that no one but whites populated these new communities was offensive to him. Many of the farmhands going back to the early settlements of the 1800s were African Americans. Those who tilled the land knew the land. It was a part of them as it was a part of Roy's family, the difference being he owned the deed.

Roy Sr. would sell a portion of his land, but not to William Levitt. This was neither charity nor an act of philanthropy. It was business. A group of black entrepreneurs paid more than market value but far less than William Levitt was offering. Roy Sr. wanted a good steward and he got it.

But the modern world had snuck up on the peaceful villages, hamlets, and small towns of Long Island. There was no turning back and Roy Sr. knew it. Before his death he told his son, "Don't sell another inch of our land. Fight to keep it as our ancestors fought to survive on it. If you sell our land, you've sold a part of us. Most importantly, continue sharing it with others, so they don't forget what this place truly is." His dying words were words to live by. And so Roy did.

His parents now long gone and his wife in the nursing home, he wondered what would become of the place his family called home. He had honored his father's request. Not a single inch of land had been sold. Now in the twilight of his own life, he asked what would become of the farm.

He stopped the tractor, stepped off, and pulled a few blades of fescue grass from the hard soil and held them in his hands. Would this grass be replaced by concrete? He looked toward the hay barn that once held hay, then wood, and now his aged airplane. He looked toward the large dairy barn where he once milked cows and performed his daily chores, now the wind its only inhabitant. Every look brought another memory. *Who will make the new memories? he asked himself. Who?*

What are we, but for our memories? Roy had not been one to live in the past, but his age and Sarah's Alzheimer's brought him to look back instead of forward. He closed his eyes, the narcotic of reminiscence bathing him with twilight's last gleaming. Deer were present only in memory, but he could see a herd of them foraging on acorns and flowered plants at the farm's forest edge. He could hear a mix of people, young and old, neighbor and stranger alike, city folk on a weekend country drive who found the farm by accident, their curiosity and discovery as sweet as the apple pie in their picnic basket. They parked, spread a blanket, and ate among the deer. Roy and Sarah welcomed all.

He opened his eyes and it was the same place in present day as it was in his memory. Age bestows wisdom to the ignorant as well as the wise. Perhaps, he thought, those who don't want to see are free of the pain from those who do. Then, you may ask, who is the wiser? People may have come and gone, but he knew, as all farmers know, that nothing lasts forever except the earth and sky. *Concrete has no business here!* seethed the frail, frightened man.

Roy collected himself, mounted the tractor, and turned over the diesel engine, the rhythmic vibration of the engine and the smell of the diesel exhaust as familiar as anything he'd known. It calmed him, comforted him. He put the tractor in gear and continued in his work as he had done his entire life.

CHAPTER 7

amphitheatrum flavium

JEREMY HEARD THE GRUNT of the diesel engine before he saw the yellow school bus turn the corner and roll to a stop. He wished for a flat tire, for an overheated engine, or that Blaze, the bus driver who always smelled of stale cigarettes and whose eyes were as bloodshot as the brake lights, would be pulled over for speeding . . . for a fourth time. Wishing and luck drew from the same river, and for Jeremy, that body of water was as putrid as the San Souci Swamp.

The door clanked open and Jeremy noticed the logo above it—a blackbird, its wings spread as if it were trying to free itself from the metal cage that Jeremy was now about to enter. *Maybe he's not going to school today. Maybe he's onto other prey. Maybe he turned into a nice person. If not today, tomorrow. Why postpone the beating?* Jeremy knew what waited as he walked up the steps to the discordant clamor of teenage riff.

No seats in the front, damn. Little Jimmy and his crew of hyenas howled and barked as their prey entered the kill zone. They'd seen him at school, but Jeremy was too smart to be cornered. *Not on this day. Should have walked, should have walked. Don't show your fear.*

Little Jimmy, as he was known to his detractors (and as Big Mac to his crew), had only one interest in school. James Patrick

McDonough came from privilege, studied little, and earned the best grades. It wasn't academics, athletics, or following his father to Yale that moved him. Big Mac wanted more than his fellow students' attention—he wanted a cult following, a devoted flock to do what he wished without question. He wanted to be a teenage idol, but was without the looks, talent, or charisma of a celebrity who was loved instead of feared.

His method was simple. He'd ask you once to be part of his crew. You never knew why, but it was, as students described, the "offer you couldn't refuse." Those self-respecting boys who said no and thought good morals, virtue, and the due diligence of the school administration would carry the day soon found out how wrong they were. A good left hook and a straight right were far more valuable. Big Mac pounded on them in public spectacles. His stocky frame, Scottish temperament, and a lifetime of beatings by four older brothers had honed his fighting skills. No fight lasted more than a few seconds, with Big Mac always throwing the first punch and always the victor. Eventually they all became his devout lemmings.

Jeremy was of particular interest to Big Mac. He tried to beat fear and hate into him, but outwardly Jeremy only showed indifference. Other students watched as Jeremy dusted off, took measure of his scrapes and bruises, and continued with his day. Jeremy bled blood, but never shame, and this earned him a perverse respect in the distorted mind of the bully. He simply could not get to him. His power to bully, intimidate, and cast fear simply held no weight with Jeremy—or so that was what Jeremy led him and others to believe. Because he, too, was of the animal kingdom and could lie in wait as well.

What does a bully do when he has no power? He feeds you to his lemmings and finds new meat. Their beatings were far worse than from the hands of their leader, as they feared being beaten in turn for a job poorly done.

It had been six months since his last encounter with Big Mac, and Jeremy knew this reunion would not be a joyful one. "Hey, buddy. Where you been?" Big Mac asked with his devilish smile. He slammed Jeremy into the bus's bench seat and pressed his knee into his prey's empty stomach. Jeremy didn't believe in polite conversation when being beaten and just stared back.

The spectacle began with the roar of the crowd. "You're going to say something this time, you little shit, or you're going to eat your teeth for breakfast," Mac insisted. Jeremy covered up, deflecting the vicious blows directed toward his face. He blocked a few more punches with his arms, but the weighty kneeing to the chest caused him to groan. Jeremy's audible pain seemed to excite Big Mac, who landed a crushing hook to Jeremy's ribs. But Jeremy refused to drop his guard—bruises to the body could be hidden; those to the face had to be explained, and he had no desire to enter another confrontation with his mom or the principal.

The small space between seats and the high backrests made for excellent cover for Jeremy's left and right flanks. Unfortunately, it also made it impossible for Blaze, the bus driver, to see the goings-on in the back of the bus. Not that he much cared. Jeremy fended off a barrage of punches but knew it was a matter of time before one of three things happened: the bus arrived at school, Mac gave up, or the punches got through.

"Say something, you shit, or I won't stop," Mac gasped, his sweat dripping from his chin onto Jeremy's arm. With one final frustrated attempt, Big Mac threw a jumping left hook that caught Jeremy square on the left side of his lower chin and mouth. The bitter taste of blood filled his mouth and he saw a flash of light. Mac's lemmings howled in delight.

"Say something or I'll hit you again!" Mac said. Nothing. Not a word. Jeremy stared resolutely, his mouth filled with blood, his defenses down, and Mac a blur hovering over him. For the first time

Jeremy thought of saying something, but what to say? *Give in. Surrender.* His mind raced and his first thoughts were of his mom, of the swamp, of her. He wanted to yell her name and again the urge surprised him. He gestured for Mac to come closer.

"Everyone speaks in the end, even the mulatto bastard," Mac said. "He speaks!" Caesar exclaimed to the seated Roman crowd. Mac leaned in and the crowd quieted. "Tell me who's your bitch, mulatto. Tell me—"

Jeremy spewed a mouthful of blood and spit into Mac's face, from the depths of his bruised abdomen and propelled by hate. Blinded by the wave of slobber, Mac staggered back. Jeremy leaped toward the front of the bus and in one movement opened the door and was gone, Blaze oblivious to all except the waving women at the red light.

Jeremy ran past the back of the bus and into oncoming traffic. Seeing the flashing red lights of the school bus, motorists slowed as Jeremy swiftly weaved his way between them. This time he left not a trail of mud and swamp water, but droplets of his blood splattering on the hoods of cars.

Like wounded prey Jeremy was running from the hunter, and only fate kept him from being hit by a passing truck. Every step he took radiated pain in his swollen face as if he were being hit again and again.

Jeremy scanned the blurred horizon and fixed upon the place he went when things got tough. It wasn't his mother's basement apartment or the comfort of a friend's home. He had no friends. No cell phone. No computer. No tweets. No text messages. No emails. But he had one thing they did not. It was his safe place, his shelter from the world, and no one knew of it but him and him alone.

In a full sprint, he never looked back or slowed down. His lungs screamed for him to stop, his heart hammered against his ribs as if it wanted to escape his chest as he had escaped from the bus. His hands were heavy, his face ablaze in the cold, cutting wind. The weight of the world split his shoulders, but he ran and ran. Big Mac wasn't chasing him. Jeremy knew this. Mac chased no one. The bully would have his revenge, but not on this day.

Jeremy raced for the bay. He sprinted across the railroad tracks, ducked between pedestrians shopping on Main Street, and crossed the lush yards of Victorian homes built in the 1920s. Few noticed, and those who did took no interest. Passing the Bayport Marina, his heated lungs now tasted brine, salt, and seaweed, the land finally giving way to the choppy waters of the Great South Bay. Towering golden reed grass swayed in symphony with the wind as Jeremy looked for the crooked tree rising from the dense grass along the seashore. Buried in the sloping dunes amongst the catbrier and Indian grass, the cedar pitch pine stood just above the tops of the reeds. If you walked directly into the forest of foliage—and no one ever did—it opened up to a space Jeremy called his own, a tree house on the beach, his castle in the sand.

He wondered how the pitch pine got there. How it survived. Alone, year after year, undeterred by the harsh winters, its roots fed by waters from land and sea. Of one, of both, of neither. To survive on what the world feeds you even if it's shit. To carry on for yet another day.

The dense foliage provided cover from beachgoers just a few yards away. And on those days when he wasn't the prey and his imagination broke free from the muck of the world and his eyes saw beyond his own misery, he climbed to the top of the curved tree. His head perched just above the swaying reed grass, he took in the vast expanse of the bay. He was the captain of his ship, surveying the seascape. And like a passing thought, sailboats gently moved across the horizon as speedboats ruptured the smooth fabric of the bay's surface. But not on this day.

Jeremy headed for the tree and disappeared into the tall reed grass. In the midst of his sand castle he sat down, exhausted by another day of . . . survival. This time he didn't laugh. He cried himself to sleep, his salty tears making their way through the sand back to the waters of the Great South Bay. Because we are all of the sea.

CHAPTER 8

mac and cheese

HE COULD FEEL HER WAITING. Her life as he knew it was one big wait, and for what he didn't know. Perhaps for me to leave so she could get on with her life. Jeremy entered the basement apartment and saw a mix of relief and anger on Clare's face. In the relief he saw love, in her anger he saw the burden of his existence. Yes, love. She cares, and this is the way she shows it. Adults, friggin' adults. Here we go.

"Where have you been? The school called! They asked me if you were sick."

"What did you tell them?"

"I told them the truth."

"The truth—that's a first for you!" Jeremy spat.

Clare's anger propelled her from the couch in one furious motion. Face to face with her son, she realized that she no longer towered over her son. This surprised her. For a fleeting second it gave reference to her life and the life they shared. *Where had all the years gone? Who is this child in front of me?*

At fourteen, he now stood as her equal, at least in height. They stared at each other, her anger revealed by a tightened upper lip and flush red skin. Jeremy was unmoved.

"Where were you?"

"I got into a fight on the bus and never made it to school."

"You didn't come home!"

"I didn't want to get into another fight."

"I'm not fighting with you!"

"Then why are you shouting?"

"This is a mother asking where her son was all day! I have that right, damn it!" Love takes many forms, and expressed at the end of a pointed finger was love nonetheless.

"I should have come home. I'm sorry."

"Who did this? Was it the same boy I called the school about last time?"

"Yes."

"What the hell are they doing at that school?"

"He's just a harmless thug."

"Harmless? Look at your face. You're not starting fights, are you, Jeremy?"

"Yeah, Mom. I'm the bully."

"I'm not saying that. Just stay away from him. I'll call the school again tomorrow."

"Lot of good that will do."

Clare turned away and threw her hands up. "Your grades, and now this—fighting and cutting class. What am I to do, Jeremy? What am I to do?" She turned back to Jeremy and he watched her anger turn to guilt. She touched his swollen jaw like only a mother could.

"Go to your room and clean up. I'll make you some mac and cheese."

He walked to his room. His mouth still tasted of iron, and he wondered if it would make dinner even less appealing. Maybe more, who knows? He knew she would serve it with love, the same love he felt for her.

She walked to the kitchen, her son's unexpected growth spurt reminding her of his father. And for the first time since Jeremy's birth she knew how distant she had become from Jeremy and the life she imagined when she was his age.

CHAPTER 9

last third

AMID A CADRE OF SOCIAL MISFITS, Jeremy and Big Mac sat silently in the school cafeteria. The smell of ammonia and floor wax signaled that the day was over even for the school janitor. Not, however, for the unruly.

Clare had kept her word and called Principal Young, but as happened many times before, both were found equally guilty and sentenced to a week's worth of detention. Knowing their history, Principal Young interviewed both and warned of serious consequences if this happened again.

At noon the cafeteria served soggy, tasteless pizza and now at day's end, a slice of imprisonment. All detainees, as the gym teacher Mr. Turner called them, had to serve the required two hours of detention in complete silence, or their sentence would be extended at his discretion. Far more torturous than the enforced silence were the lectures. Not that Turner wanted to be here any more than they did, but it was his week in the "lunchbox," as the teachers called it.

"School detention is a gateway to future incarceration," he told his captive audience. "This place is a reflection of your future."

"You mean our future is in the food business, Warden Turner?"

Big Mac yelled, to the other misfits' laughter.

"Not funny, James Patrick McDonough," Turner said.

Jeremy looked out the window, his eyes following a small plane crossing the setting sun. Stearman. *That crazy old man is chasing the sun over the next ridge. Take me away from this madness, you old goat.*

"I've been at this long enough to know that one third of your classmates will go to the best colleges, become well-respected and highly paid professionals and pillars of society," Turner intoned. "The second third will become government employees, teachers, nurses, construction workers, businessmen or women and live a comfortable and/or prosperous life. Trouble will be the only accomplishment of the last third, and they will be subject to the rules of the first two thirds."

"Sounds like a caste system to me," a misfit said.

"A caste system that you create for yourself, not one that you're born into. So from which third do you aspire to?"

"Hey Jeremy, aren't you in the last third?" Big Mac asked. "A bastard zebra from a welfare mom living in a basement apartment?"

"Enough!" Turner roared. "That's another day of detention, McDonough!"

Again the misfits laughed as Jeremy continued to look out the window. Stearman had disappeared over the horizon. The well of anger sat heavy in his gut like the processed lunch meat he'd eaten a few hours before in the same seat. No longer could he hold onto his sense of indignation and anger. He didn't move, he didn't let it show. Because he, too, was of the animal kingdom and could lie in wait as well. *Not my mother. Me, fine, but not her. They don't believe me or her because of who we are. We're not one of them. She tried. I tried.* Jeremy was well past the dread of punishment. He was the loser in a fixed game of Monopoly. Their rules, their way, and the game never ended.

Principal Young had a PhD in philosophy, but philosophical discourse was not part of the job description. Being a principal was more like being a boxing referee and police detective. He had the skills of neither. His PhD had failed to teach him that violence and deception are not the sole domain of the adult. Children can lie as well as or better than adults. They can be as violent and as cruel.

When students got in trouble, Principal Young spoke to them in a firm but compassionate way. His mistake was espousing Kant, not realizing that Machiavelli ruled the day. Before he had interviewed students who witnessed the beating, Big Mac had already gotten to them. Their story line was consistent but false, orchestrated like a symphony. Mac, the conductor, even claimed he was the victim. He would have gotten away scot-free but for Jeremy's bruised face. Both pugilists, as Principal Young saw fit, had to serve time.

No more. No more. I'm done, Jeremy decided, preparing for his final act as a student at James Monroe Middle School. He picked up his hard-covered math textbook, thick as a ream of paper and as hard as a brick.

When the laughter settled and the room quieted, Jeremy rose from his chair with his math book firmly in hand and calmly walked to Big Mac's desk. Mac looked up from his iPhone to see Jeremy standing over him. Their eyes met. Mac saw the rage and then a flash of light. The violent collision of the textbook against Big Mac's face made a loud crack like a tree snapping in the wind. His nose broke in three places, the force of the blow creating a whiplash, the momentum smashing his face against the desk. Blood flew in all directions as did his teeth, one spinning to Turner's foot nearly fifteen feet away.

Big Mac was a tough kid, but this time the laws of bullying were against him. As Mac had told his lemmings, "Always get the first and last shot." But on this day he would have neither. Jeremy landed the second blow clean against Mac's left temple, rupturing his eardrum and destroying the inner workings of his left ear. Membranes separated from ear, teeth from gum, bone from skin, and blood from body.

Mac crumpled to the floor with a thud and a whimper. Thick red blood spread across the linoleum tile.

Jeremy jumped on top of him and, with the skill of a farmer using a pickax to break up the earth, pummeled his face to a bloody pulp. "Last third! Last third!" Jeremy screamed as Turner and some of the other misfits tried to pull him away. "This bastard child is last third!"

Chapter 10

the final frontier

Jeremy stood motionless on the sidewalk, his arms parallel to the ground, his body casting a shadow upon the pavement like Jesus on the cross. The police officer, with wand in hand, started by Jeremy's right foot and circled his body counterclockwise.

Every day the first test at Frontier Academy was metal detection. And for those who failed, the pat down. Frontier Academy, a "last chance" public school, was staffed by hardened teachers and has-been police officers who roamed the well-secured campus of what the school system classified as an "opportunity" school. Kids with criminal records or who had been kicked out of multiple schools were sent to Frontier, their last opportunity to complete their public education. Jeremy was fortunate to be there.

"In the hands of a young adult a textbook is a weapon, a weapon to open up the magnificence of this world through knowledge—not the skull of another student. Where were the adults, the people we entrust with our kids, when my client was victimized by this vicious bully?" the lawyer had exclaimed with television cameras rolling and James Wilson Middle School as a backdrop.

Big Mac's Wall Street dad had hired a powerful Manhattan lawyer, ensuring Jeremy's conviction and costing the school district a six-figure payout for negligence. With a broken nose, no front teeth, and deaf in his left ear, it took Big Mac a full school year to recover from his injuries. His nose would be straightened and front teeth replaced, but the constant hum in his ear would never leave him. It was a ring that prevented him from hearing the ridicule of those who once feared him, but a noise that would eventually drive him mad. His confident saunter had become a tentative gait, and both the intimidation and aura that came with it were now gone, and every student knew it.

With no prior criminal record, Jeremy was spared a five-year sentence at the upstate juvenile detention facility in Albany. To the astonishment of Principal Young, he became aware of the scale of Mac's terror after his lemmings spoke out against him now that they were no longer in danger. An internal school district report concluded it was an endemic failure of the entire school's staff and administration. But for Jeremy, it was too late. The school's lawyer focused on his use of the textbook as a weapon instead of the institutional failure of the school. If he had beaten Big Mac with his hands alone it would have been just another teenage scuffle, he said. Clare had no means and no lawyer to represent her son, and the school district knew this. And Big Mac's father wanted blood. He insisted that the school district prohibit Jeremy from attending regular public school ever again.

Having passed the metal detector, Jeremy was cleared to enter the school, but not with his skateboard. Just about everything at Frontier Academy was considered a possible weapon, from the skateboard Jeremy used to travel to school to hard-covered textbooks. Nothing was left to chance.

A police officer escorted Jeremy to Mr. Collins's classroom. Sitting in the corner of the windowless trailer was a plump armed guard, his skin prison white, his eyes glazed with boredom. To Jeremy's surprise, it wasn't a class of thirty rambunctious students but a dozen kids sitting quietly in various states of disinterest. *That guard has half a chance with twelve students, no chance with thirty.*

Jeremy walked to the front of the room and stood in front of Mr. Collins, who was sitting at his desk, feet up, the *New York Times* a paper curtain between him and the class, and softly snoring. Jeremy looked around the classroom and realized that many of the students recognized the new arrival. They knew what he'd done and to whom. Big Mac and Jeremy had become ghosts of each other. Jeremy became the most popular kid in James Madison Middle School, though never to be seen again, and Big Mac was a sickly shell of his former self and now simply ignored by his fellow students.

The only smiling face among the class was a young girl in the corner of the room. She waved Jeremy over and pointed to the seat next to hers. The security guard watched the scene unfold and nodded in cautious approval.

"Don't I have to check in with him?" he asked the girl with untamed fiery red hair and deep green eyes.

"After he's done reading the paper he'll figure it out. He's on the Life section," she said. Jeremy looked around and shook his head in disbelief.

"I know, how did you get here?" she said. "We've all asked ourselves the very same question. My name is Kelli."

"Jeremy," he replied softly.

"Nice to meet you, LT."

"LT?"

"Last Third," she said with a smile. Jeremy was taken aback by the descriptive and swallowed uncomfortably, thinking about his newfound infamous nickname.

"You know why I'm here—what are you in for?" he asked.

"In for? This isn't prison. You're free to leave whenever you like."

"You could have fooled me. Full body search, armed cops,

barbed-wire fence, cell-block nicknames."

Kelli slid her seat away from her desk and unapologetically showed the bump of her belly.

"Oh," he said. "Since when do they put you in here for that?"

"I did some other stuff too. It was a hard time."

This is where life had landed Jeremy. It was a rightful punishment for a brutal act that he could never disown. One minute of rage, one loss of self-control. During all the scrums with Big Mac he defended himself and moved on, angered, yes, but an anger he always restrained. But the cut of words always stings more than the fist. The years of beatings and life itself in all its disappointments bottled up until that day. Now he knew what darkness lay within him. It brought fitful nights and greater distance between him and his mom. With one swing of the textbook, his childhood was gone.

"I'm not a criminal, Last Third," she said.

"I didn't say you were, and stop calling me that. My name is Jeremy."

"Little Jimmy had it coming. Everyone knew he'd get his someday, except those fools in charge," she said.

"I guess, but I never thought it would be me," he said.

"You think any of us thought we'd be here?"

Jeremy again looked around the room. This group was the best of the worst from all over the school district, the graduating class of the cafeteria clan. Another group of misfits, just a bit more violent and a lot more creative than those he'd left at James Madison Middle School. Now he was one of them.

Kelli pointed at them one by one and they acknowledged their discretion with a salute, a smile, or a middle finger.

"Fought the principal. Bit his teacher's ass. Blew up the principal's car. Set fire to his home room class. Sex in the back of the classroom. Put laxatives in the school's ranch dressing. Pissed in the back of the gym. Grabbed his physics teacher's breasts. Shit on a teacher's desk. Threw someone out of a window."

"Out the—"

"Second floor. Kid lived," she said dispassionately. "Yep, you're one of us."

"No, I'm not," he said.

"You keep thinking that and you'll be out of here."

"That might not be a bad thing."

"Go ahead," she said. "Leave. They won't stop you."

"Really?"

"Yep. There are three ways out of here, and they're all through the front door. You quit and walk out. You get into a fight—"

"What if someone—"

Kelli smirked. "Nobody's gonna mess with *you*. They know who you are. And everyone's afraid of everybody else around here. It ain't called Frontier for nothing. If you can't make it here, you're definitely lost in the woods."

"And what's the third way?"

"Through the front door with a degree, douchebag."

Collins woke himself up with a loud snore and lowered the curtain. "You the new convict?" he asked.

"I—"

"I'd appreciate if you checked with me before you sat down."

"You were snoring," Jeremy replied. "I didn't want to interrupt you."

Collins shot a loathing glance at the security guard. "Come here," he said.

Jeremy walked up to his desk and stood in front of him.

"I don't need some convict lecturing me on how I do my job," Collins said. Jeremy did not reply.

"Take a seat, turn on the computer, and it will explain everything. You do know how to read?"

"I do."

"Good. How 'bout turning on a computer?"

"I do."

"How 'bout 'yes' instead of 'I do.' What, are you getting married? Now go sit next to Kelli, she seems to be the only adult among you . . . students. If you get stuck ask her. She's practicing her maternal instincts. Now I know you don't know what maternal means. Correct?"

"I do n—"

"You'll find out," Collins interrupted. "Go."

Jeremy walked back to his seat, looked at Kelli, and shook his head. "Real winner that guy."

Kelli responded with a cold glance and returned to her work.

Collins was born too late—late was the story of his life. His hippie parents were there for it all: Nixon, Vietnam, the March on Washington, the beginning of the environmental movement. In '55 they met, had Frank William Collins, and as quickly as he was born gave him up to his grandmother and hit the road, the first wave of what would turn into the sixties movement. By the time they had finally settled in a quiet Ohio neighborhood twenty years later, Frank had long since understood that the tenets of history always have a cost—in his case, the loss of a decent childhood.

At first he hated them, but he understood they were part of history, part of something bigger, a history he would study in college and proudly teach his students. What he hated was present day. The world his parents and their generation dreamed of was now a vulgar, tasteless world of suburban apathy. A generation of indifference. The kids he was to inspire and help unearth their own dreams knew little of the civil rights marches, the antiwar protests, or the environmental movement. He tried to motivate his students to the rich history of the cause. But they didn't listen. They simply didn't care. Today's youth, he believed, were anesthetized with consumerism and selfishness.

They were convicts to unabashed capitalism.

Collins was equally angry at his own generation. They had created the very world his parents had railed against and had gotten rich doing so. Both cynical and poor, Collins failed on both counts. His last vestige of protest was his ponytail, but with thinning hair, eyes too small for his head, and an angry demeanor, he looked like a man who life had passed up. Frontier Academy was his last school before retirement. His only interest was the countdown. Like most teachers at Frontier, he sat reading the newspaper and mumbling under his breath at the failings of the world.

Occasionally Collins would walk around and assist students, since they were prohibited from interacting with each other. Kelli was the exception. The biology of pregnancy has its dictates, discomfort being one of many, and Kelli was free to roam the class, knowing that Collins and the security guard had enough sense not to annoy a pregnant teenager.

The obsolete computer bolted to the desk was as unwelcoming as Jeremy's new teacher. He failed to find the on switch until a hand flipped it on from the back. He thanked Kelli, but she threw him an angry stare. He didn't know if it was for interrupting her studies or his judgmental stare when she proudly showed her distended belly. The computer opened with the school logo, and Jeremy wondered if the sun over the bright red horizon was setting or rising. The machine asked for a password and he typed LASTTHIRD.

UNABLE, the computer responded. Minimum eight characters, numbers and letters, no spaces.

He tried again. LASTTHIRD3.

Accepted.

It was his first day of school in eight months.

Chapter 11

to the end of the world
with you

Jeremy looked out upon the bay from his castle in the sand, not knowing what to think about his first day of school, how the campus was surrounded by razor-wire, and the girl with the fiery red hair who'd shown him more kindness and consideration than he deserved. No one had ever spoken to him like that. So directly, so matter-of-fact with no wasted words. *What's her angle, what does she want from me?*

Jeremy knew strife and nothing more and hoped for some semblance of normalcy to return to his life. He'd had his fill of juvenile courts, lawyers, judges, and cops and just wanted to be left alone. That he'd never return to James Wilson Middle School was fine with him. Life as presently served would have to do.

He drew in the comfort of the salty sea air and exhaled the pain of the last eight months. He missed his beach castle and had enjoyed tidying the place up after his long absence. His heart lifted when he peered through the reed grass and saw that it was still there. He thought the sea might have swallowed it during his absence, as he knew that nothing lasts forever except the earth, the sky, and "that place" across the bay. It was the only subject he'd ever researched, and it was never far from his thoughts. He called it Seal Island, as the Algonquin did. The name would disappear, as did the seals and eventually the Algonquin, but what's in a name? The Dutch and English settlers named it the Barrier Island, but the best of names, the most appropriate and most spiritual of names, are always given by the natives. Fire Island. *What's over there?* he asked himself the first time his mother spoke of it and well before he cast eyes upon it.

The Great South Bay was the destination for some, but for others it was Fire Island, a narrow strip of land that underlined Long Island like the tail end of a fancy signature. But for Jeremy, it was always his castle in the sand, his home, and never "that place." He tried to ignore Seal Island, but his imagination always followed his eyes like his shadow followed his person, because he knew that the island was for real moms, real dads, and kids enjoying long summer days, eating hot dogs and hamburgers off the grill, and it was where macaroni and cheese did not exist.

Jeremy drew his hands across the tall reeds that defined his castle walls. Their innocence had been lost, made adult by an act of violence. He remembered the day they were splattered with Big Mac's blood. What will become of me? He had no answer, and his mother had all but stopped asking. It wasn't that she gave up on him. Hope springs eternal in the breast of every mother, no matter what the circumstance.

Called to the school after the attack, she did what all moms do, defending her son as if her own life were being judged. It was. Taken to the Fifth Precinct and shown photos of James Patrick McDonough, Clare fell to the floor as if she had been hit by Jeremy himself. She held her head in her hands, but they didn't hold back the tears. The detectives from the Fifth Precinct and the female officer from child services looked at her as if she was the cause.

Big Mac's name was never mentioned. His behavior was irrelevant. "Poor parental child rearing," they said. "A single-parent household, a child raised in poverty with inadequate supervision and low attachment." She could not deny the "facts" of their case and was too traumatized to defend herself. The clinical psychologist diagnosed Jeremy as having a "propensity" for violence and an IQ in the below-average range.

Through the catbrier and Indian grass, Jeremy watched as people walked along the beach. He saw lovers holding hands, families picnicking on the sand, mothers tickling their giggling babies: the simple acts of people who share their love.

Jeremy noticed an elderly couple at the water's edge. Hand in hand, they stood facing each other. Among the beachgoers they stood alone, her eyes opaque, her movements rigid; his touch gentle, his look comforting. She didn't smile and looked confused. Then he sang:

> *A wonderful power has entered my life,*
> *It came when your eyes reached my heart.*
> *I live in a glorious dreamland with you,*
> *A kingdom of love set apart,*
> *And all of my joys are because I love you,*
> *For love is my life and my all,*
> *And ages to be, only mean you to me,*
> *To love until heaven's roll call.*
> *Tho' stars of hope are burning low, dear,*
> *And all the world is filled with woe, dear,*
> *My heart will bid me to go dear,*
> *To the end of the world with you!*

At song's end, she smiled a lover's smile, her eyes if only for a moment fixed and clear on her husband.

And Jeremy smiled a child's smile.

Chapter 12

fly or fall

THE SUN WARMED THE CRISP spring air, making his lunch of frankfurters and soggy fries seem almost like a picnic. Jeremy sat alone on the grass leaning against the razor wire–topped perimeter fence.

"Are you going to eat that?" Kelli asked. Jeremy hadn't seen Kelli walk over. He looked up to see her eying his half-eaten hot dog.

"Sure, take it."

She sat down, and in two easy bites it was gone. "I haven't been this hungry in my life. Thanks."

"You're welcome. The other day, I apologize—"

"For what?"

"What I called you."

"You didn't call my anything."

"In my mind I did."

Kelli laughed. "Care to share?"

"Nope."

"I bet I've been called a lot worse. I'll accept your apology if you give me your ice cream sandwich."

"That I will share with you." Jeremy broke his ice cream sandwich in half and offered her the strawberry side.

"The vanilla side," Kelli said.

"Nope. Vanilla is my favorite. We all have our limits."

"That we do." Both smiled.

"So why aren't you afraid of me?" Jeremy asked.

"Fear is overrated. Getting to know people takes effort, sometimes courage. And when you have courage, you discover things about yourself too."

Jeremy took a bite out of his vanilla sandwich. Two caged students enjoying a midday feeding. Her honesty and blunt talk was as refreshing as the ice cream sandwich, yet his suspicion of others was always present. *What's her angle? She wants something. Sex?*

"So what are you saying?" he asked. "If I get to know you I'll know myself better?"

"Maybe. I can see it in your eyes."

"See what?"

"That cursor on your computer hasn't moved since you got here. You're unfocused, too distracted."

Jeremy barked out a nervous laugh. "It's my second week. Cut me a break."

"You don't need any more breaks. You're broken enough. We all are."

"I didn't mean—"

"Have you asked yourself why that cursor hasn't moved?"

He hadn't asked himself. He searched hopelessly for an answer, and then he was saved by the ring of the lunch bell.

Kelli stood up. "Thanks for the food," she said, and walked away.

❖   ❖   ❖

At day's end with skateboard firmly underfoot, Jeremy pushed off from school. He chewed on Kelli's lunchtime conversation like cud.

Screw her.

The short school buses had fewer routes than those at the regular school, and none close to his basement apartment, so Jeremy relied on his skateboard. No kickflips or ollies, no slides, no grinds. He wasn't a skater, didn't hang out at the local skate park and never wanted to. His board was another gift from his grandparents given to him by his mother. For him it was a poor substitute for his bicycle, transportation and nothing more.

He could hear Kelli's voice as the urethane wheels rolled over the rough cement sidewalk, jarring both mind and body. His thoughts rolled together as he pushed down the road. He couldn't focus. He was distracted. And the cursor didn't move.

I feel old. It felt like a dozen birthdays had passed since his beating of Big Mac. *It takes courage.* Jeremy pushed on, trying to quiet her voice and enjoy the late afternoon commute back home.

He loved being on the move. The sidewalk leading home had one section where it paralleled a long perimeter fence just like the one at Frontier. The fence was eight feet tall with razor wire at the top with signs every fifty feet: AUTHORIZED PERSONNEL ONLY. RESTRICTED AREA. This time he was on the outside looking in at a great expanse of grass and the beginnings of what looked like a runway.

Good cement. Board speed! No one can catch me. No one can find me. No one can corner me. Freedom! He could hear the crickets hiding in the deep foliage chirping and the wind whistling in his ears.

He saw it before he heard it, its shark-like shadow passing before him. His eyes skyward, the large jet quickly roared by overhead. He could see its dirty underbelly and the rivets that kept its guts together. His internal organs shook and his eardrums shuddered to the shattered static of the engines' roar.

He felt it before he saw it. Bam! Headfirst into the fence, both board and boy tumbling to the ground. He laughed, familiar with the aches, pains, and bruises of bike speed and now the terrible indignity of skateboard speed. Undeterred, Jeremy dusted himself off, laughed, and got up. With a slight cut above his eye trickling blood into his brow, he pressed his bruised face against the fence. He watched and waited for the next plane, and the next and the next. They flew overhead every three minutes, shaking him to his core, each plane as deafening and as grand as the last. They drew him outside himself, away from his strangely comforting world of blood and bruises. He was fascinated that something so large, so loud, and so lumbering could stay in the air and gently return back to earth. Each time he laughed a little more until he screamed in delight. "Now that's freedom!" he yelled.

He hadn't thought much, if at all, about Stearman, but wondered now if he was piloting the big airplanes overhead. *Crazy old goat.*

◆　◆　◆

In dreams some fly, some fall, and some do both. Jeremy laid his head on the pillow, remembering the planes landing before him that afternoon. It comforted him as he drifted into sleep. His stomach heavy with mac and cheese, he knew his dream life wouldn't be as pleasant, but on this night he hoped that he would carry the smile and joy of the afternoon with him. Even in sleep, life poked and gnawed at him. He could not remember a night of deep, uninterrupted sleep, only of nights awakening to the dark thoughts of his cheek pressed against the cafeteria's linoleum floor and drowning in a sea of Big Mac's blood.

This night would be different. As he faded into a slumber, Kelli appeared in his dream. Standing outside his castle in the sand, he could barely see her through the reed grass. *What are you doing here?* She said nothing and extended her hands through the vegetation that defined the castle walls. But these were not her hands. These were neither the hands of a sixteen year old nor a fourteen year old but of a newborn. Covered in dew, the small hands were sprinkled with seeds born from the flowers high atop the reed grass. Jeremy watched as the small fingers wiggled and clasped at the air as if to grab it before clenching helplessly into a fist. He looked up through the long vines and both were suddenly gone. He was relieved, but this was a dream where no one and no thing were ever gone. Her voice resonated through his castle:

> See my hands reaching out tonight
> Hear my words they are dynamite
> See how they light your way tonight.
> See your hands reaching out tonight.

Fly or fall. Find your way tonight. He woke up reaching for her hands and a memory rudely took the place of dream. The Fifth Precinct jail cell after his arrest. He longed for his castle on the beach, but all he saw were the walls of cold concrete bricks lit in jailhouse florescence. He heard the desperate yells of others, directed to no one but perhaps their helpless selves. Jeremy longed to cry out, to wail like the others, but to whom? The thought of his mom flickered and then was quickly gone.

The prison cell didn't smell of sea salt or brine, nor was it warmed by the heat of a sunny summer day. A small vent next to the open metal toilet provided heat and wafted the smell of bleach and Pine-Sol. *The school cafeteria. It smells like the school cafeteria.* A chuckle and a memory opened a door leading to another. He heard the voice of Mr. Turner—"From which group do you belong; to which group do you aspire?"

What he missed most was the view, the view from the castle, of people walking the beach, bathers in knee-deep water, boats resting upon the bay's belly, sailboats destined for that distant shore—"that place." Prison took away the horizon and with that all possibilities. Jeremy grew to hate even the thought of Fire Island until it was taken away. And for the first time in his young life, he wanted to go there. He did not ask why, but he knew why as she knew why.

I got you thinking. Now ask yourself why? It takes courage.

CHAPTER 13

american harvester

IN THEIR PRIME, Roy and his tractor could work the yoke out of an entire day, from before sunrise to after sunset. But in the twilight of both their lives, Roy respectfully babied the aged but reliable tractor by running it only in the cool temperatures of early morning or late afternoon. And on this day, like so many days in his long life, it in turn helped Roy complete the task of bush-hogging the many acres of farm grass.

With the long shadows of late afternoon greeting the last line of fescue, Roy turned the tractor 180 degrees, lined the inside wheel with the high grass, and stepped on the accelerator. He looked up. Fifty yards in front of him, directly in the path of the last line of grass, stood . . . that kid. Not imagined. Real. *What the hell does he want?* Roy stepped on the accelerator.

Jeremy stood statue-like as the hungry red bull began its charge. It grunted and growled, spewing black smoke and kicking up grass as it sped toward him. *Should I run away or stand my ground?* To run with the bulls of Pamplona or stand in front of the tank like the man in Tienanmen Square? Running assured survival, but he was done running. His legs began to shake as the tractor closed in. Roy locked eyes with this bizarre kid with strange hair and copper skin.

Christ, I'll be cut to pieces and mixed with cow shit! I'll be shit just like everyone says I am! The roar of the tractor shook the ground and reverberated in Jeremy's chest cavity as it closed in. He could smell the carbureted gas and see the cut grass sticking to the tires. He could read the flat-white, weathered lettering on top of the grill: AMERICAN HARVESTER.

I'll scare the shit out of him. Damn kids today don't respect their elders, Roy thought. How one would do this with a two-ton tractor was something that Roy had not fully thought through—gunboat diplomacy from the blunt end of a tractor.

Soft brakes, the evening dew, and the old man's declining reflexes all made for a bad summit. Roy hit the brakes a bit too late, the brakes grabbed a tad too slow, and the wet grass was as smooth as ice.

"Oh, sh—" Jeremy closed his eyes, turned his head, and threw up his arms parallel to the ground. His body cast a long shadow on the grass, not of Jesus on the cross but of the Scarecrow in Oz. The thud of raw meat hitting the floor could be heard over the sound of the tractor's engine. The confidence of self was knocked out of him, along with every ounce of air, as the grill of the tractor hit him square from groin to chest.

This was much different than falling from his bike. It was as if the very essence of life had been ripped out of him. His body spun upward toward the crisp orange hue of the setting sun. Floating in the air, he thought he was dead, his lungs vacant, his chest heavy, but then as quickly as they had been emptied, his body reclaimed the spent air. He drew a deep breath: his chest painfully expanded, his brain awoke, and life returned. Life, however, quickly turned to black when he hit the ground a few yards in front of the snarling bull with a heavy thump.

"Kid! Kid! Kid!" Roy pleaded. He shook Jeremy, but the boy lay motionless in the uncut fescue grass. "Kid! Kid! Please be alive!" Roy pleaded.

Jeremy's unfocused eyes looked skyward to the haze of the old man's frightful face.

"Kid—you all right? Is anything broken?"

"Fi . . . Is . . ."

"Kid, kid, you all right? What are you saying?"

"Fir . . . Isl . . ." Jeremy replied.

"I don't understand."

"Fire Isla . . ." Jeremy replied, his senses slowly returning.

"Fire? There's no fire here."

"Fire Is . . . land."

"Fire Island? This is Long Island. You might have a concussion."

Jeremy's pupils came into focus, the fog slowly started to lift, and he realized what had happened. "You're a cra . . . zy old go . . . at! You could have ki . . . lled me!" Jeremy tried to get up, but his head throbbed and body felt like a sack of water. "Fire Island, you old shit!" he yelled, making the throbbing in his head worse.

"Kid, you're not thinking right. Your brain's jello. You're not making sense. Why didn't you get out of the way?"

"Why didn't you stop, you goat's ass!"

"What the hell do you want with me?"

"I told you. Fire Island, you goatfuck!"

"Fire Island?" Roy laughed, relieved by the kid's rudeness, which he took as a sign that the boy was all right. "Take the goddamn ferry, you dumb shit!"

"I don't have enough money for the ferry, you ass of an old goat!" Jeremy said.

With every insult Roy laughed harder. This kid reminded Roy of his own years as a teenager. Jeremy rolled to his side like a boxer trying to get up from the canvas, then flopped back to the turf.

"Just stay put for a while, son, let your senses catch up with you," Roy said.

"Did you catch the setting sun?" Jeremy asked.

"What?"

"A while back you were flying in the late afternoon and you flew toward the sun. Did you catch the sun?"

"Son, you're not making any sense. Best if I take you to the hospital."

"I'm fine. Did you catch the setting sun?"

"No plane I know can catch the setting sun . . . son."

"Then why do you fly?" Jeremy asked.

Roy didn't have an answer. He had never thought about why. "Why do you need to go to Fire Island?"

"Could you fly me there? Drop me off?"

"You going to answer my question?"

"You didn't answer mine."

"Which one?" Roy asked.

"Either of them."

"I can't take you. No airstrip there."

"There's flat ground just like here."

"Landed on the beach many times, years ago. A lifetime ago. Times are different. Now it's illegal. You just can't land a plane wherever you please," Roy said.

"Why not? Planes land here all the time."

"This is my property, at least for now. Best I can do is a low pass."

Feeling slowly returned to Jeremy's legs and he stood. "Low pass? Sounds like my grades in school."

"I wasn't much of a student either. Ten feet over the beach line. Will that work?"

"No, but sounds fun."

"That it is," Roy said.

"How 'bout I do some work on your farm and you pay me?"

"Ferry?"

"Yeah."

"This isn't a working farm anymore."

"Well, isn't cutting the grass working?!" Jeremy insisted.

"No one drives my tractor."

"Why not?!"

"'Cause."

"'Cause why?!"

"'Cause I say so!" Roy yelled.

"Not good enough."

"Says who?"

"Me," Jeremy said.

"*No!* Says me! The owner of the tractor!"

"Running me over has got to be worth something!"

"Yeah, the cost of a ferry ride! What's it cost these days?"

"Nine dollars one way, seventeen round."

"Jeez, used to cost fifty cents in my day." Roy pulled out a twenty and handed it over. "Here's twenty. You keep it. This is for me almost killing you."

"Three dollars don't buy much food."

Roy laughed. "What a goat rope. Twenty-five is all you're getting,"

Jeremy took the money as quickly as it was offered. "Thank you, Mr. Stearman," Jeremy said.

"Why'd you call me that?"

"That's the name on your plane, isn't it?"

"It is, but that's not my name." He extended his hand. "Roy Higgins."

"Then who is Jack Stearman and why do you have his plane?"

Roy laughed again. "Shake hands and I'll tell you." They shook and Roy explained.

"Jeremy, right?"

"That's right."

"Why don't you head on home now?"

"Thanks again," Jeremy said appreciatively.

"You're welcome."

Jeremy slowly walked away, not running in fear as he did the first time they'd met. At a distance he looked back and waved. The gesture returned in kind, Roy climbed back onto the tractor, turned the engine over, and looked at the last few feet of uncut grass. "Well," he said to the harvester, "we've never had a mow like this." Then he headed toward the barn, leaving the last few feet of grass uncut.

CHAPTER 14

the dead sea

JEREMY SAT AT HIS DESK, the cursor on his computer blinking. He looked at Kelli as she went about her tasks with a singular focus. *She likes school. This place doesn't bother her. Nothing bothers her.* While the others wasted their days too damaged and too unfocused to help themselves, her purpose was clear: have her baby, finish school, and go to college. *How does she do it? No angle I guess, just someone to talk to and an extra lunch. She is eating for two. Who can blame her?*

The numbers were against Kelli: less than a 50 percent chance of finishing school, a 40 percent chance of living in poverty, and an 80 percent chance of being on welfare. She understood the long road ahead; her intuition needed no percentage. She knew it in her bones and in her belly. Create a new destiny or drown in the Dead Sea.

"Staring at me isn't going to help you graduate," she said without turning her head. "Do you need help?"

"No?"

"Is that a question or answer?"

"Who says I need help?"

"'Cause the cursor on your computer still hasn't moved. Do you want help?"

"I don't need help. And why would you help me?"

"Because, you can't go it alone." Kelli pointed to her belly. "I don't live at home."

"So where do you live?"

"My parents gave me a choice. Give up the baby and you can stay."

"What type of choice is that?"

"Exactly."

"So what did you do?"

"I tried going it alone and couldn't." The difficulty reflected in her voice. Those first few cold nights walking the streets, sleeping in the public bathroom by the South Bay. The inviting crashing of the sea a dark reminder of how easy it would be to end it all. She chose life and the cold cement floor of the female urinal and survived another day. But she knew what he didn't.

"There's nothing wrong with asking for help," she said.

Kelli continued working, never once looking over at Jeremy, the cursor on his computer unmoved.

◆　◆　◆

The school day over, the kids of Frontier exited the barbed-wire front gate under the watchful eye of the police. Six short buses, the ridicule of kids from the regular school, lined up beside the curb. The buses were numbered one through five. The last had the initials BW papered to the side window. Jeremy caught up with Kelli as she walked toward her bus.

"Where do you live?" he asked.

"Why do you want to know? You a stalker?" she joked.

"I don't think so?"

"I'll take that as a yes."

"You never told me where you lived and since you don't live with your parents—"

"And if I tell you and you come over uninvited, then you're a stalker."

"I promise you that won't happen," he said.

"They don't live with their parents either," Kelli said, pointing to the buses.

Jeremy looked at the short bus with the initials BW. In it were girls.

"Yep, just like me," she said.

Just like my mom. In their faces all he could see was his mom's face. *Future me's.* Future Jeremys gestating in those girls. *I'm not the only one. Mom is not the only one. There are others. How many me's are out there? God help those kids.*

"Why do you think I need help?" he asked.

"You're full of questions."

"You seem to be full of answers or full of shit. I'm trying to find out which."

"Fair enough. I see it in your eyes."

"What are you, some kinda witch?"

"Witch, bitch, whore, slut—I've been called lots of things."

"I've been called a lot of things too. So what?"

"You live with your mom, no dad, no friends, right?"

"So?" Jeremy asked defensively.

"That's a yes. You blame yourself for your mom's situation and you think her life would be better without you."

"So?"

"That's a yes too. You're a lousy student, not because you're dumb, because you're unfocused, too distracted."

Jeremy was silent. *God, she* is *a witch.*

"Again, a yes."

"And how do you think you can help me there, Miss Know It All?"

"I already have."

"*Really.*"

"Yep, I got you thinking."

"More like annoyed."

"Then why do you keep talking to someone who annoys you?" Kelli pointed to the BW sign on the bus window. "It's called Bridge Way House. It's my home, but the ignorant call it a shelter. Come on, take a ride and I'll show you."

"I can't go in there. I'm not allowed."

"Sure you are. You just have to have sex with one of us when you get to the house," she said with a wink.

"I knew it!"

"I want to have sex with you?" Kelli laughed. "So you do think I'm a slut."

"You said it, so you must be thinking it!"

"God, men are so dumb," she said, and Jeremy realized that he was. He froze, his face red and his eyes as big as oranges.

"I'll see you tomorrow and we'll chalk this conversation up to you being a dumb shit. Agreed?"

"Do I have a choice?" Jeremy mumbled.

"No."

Kelli climbed into the bus and sat next to the window facing the curb. She threw him a wave and a small smile as the bus exited the parking lot.

I'm a dumb ass. But help? My ass! She's in a worse situation than I am and she's giving me advice! Please.

Then Jeremy noticed another sign dangling from the rear window as the bus turned the corner and disappeared from sight: THIS BUS HAS BEEN CHECKED FOR SLEEPING CHILDREN.

CHAPTER 15

autocycle super de luxe

"JEREMY . . . JEREMY . . . JEREMY! Wake up!"

Jeremy was lying in his bed in that strange place between sleep and awake. He hadn't slept well as this Saturday would be the day he made his trip to Fire Island. His dreams had drawn currents from his everyday life, not traversing a story of fantasy or nightmare but of a beach of black sand and unwelcoming waves, the retreating seas leaving his Trek bicycle and backpack at water's edge, both in perfect condition. Just as he was opening the backpack, he was awakened by his mother's voice. *What was in it?*

"It's Saturday, Mom!"

"I know what day it is!" Clare said. "Who's Ass of an Old Goat?"

"What?"

"Who's Ass of an Old Goat? Who's Goat's Ass?"

"What are you talking about?" Jeremy grumbled.

"There's something on the front step I want you to see!"

"From who?"

"From *whom*! Speak properly!"

"From whom then?"

"Ass of an Old Goat."

"Who? Whom?" Jeremy pulled the sheet down and got out of

his bed.

"Oh my God!" Clare exclaimed. "What happened to you? Your chest is black and blue!"

"You should have seen it a few days ago."

"Have you been fighting again?"

"No, Mom."

"My Lord! What'd you get hit by, a car?"

"Worse," he said.

"Jesus, Mary, and Joseph! *Worse?* Really! What's worse than getting hit by a car?!"

"A tractor," he answered flippantly.

"A tractor trailer!"

"Mom, I'd be dead if I was hit by a tractor trailer. It was just a regular tractor." Jeremy took the note from her and read it as he walked to the front door, Clare closely in tow.

I figure you might need this more than I do. Every kid should have a bike. Hope you're feeling better.

Vr,

Ass of an Old Goat

Goat's Ass

Goat F—

Jeremy opened the door to the basement apartment to the late morning sun shining brightly on the cracked cement stoop.

"Holy shit!" Jeremy yelped.

"Language!" Clare said.

"Sorry. Hold on, Mom. I'll explain in a second." Jeremy was trying to take in the beauty of it, the magnificence of a Schwinn bicycle from the year 1940, his trashed backpack by its side.

AUTOCYCLE, he read on the streamlined phantom tank attached to the frame's spine. It had a front headlight built into the mudguards, a rear carrier, a horn, and a leather seat with springs underneath.

Jeremy inquisitively knocked on the frame, then picked up the bike. "This is tricked out! The cholos at school will eat it up. I wonder how it rides?" he asked himself aloud. "Heavy. It's made of steel. New tires. Everything else looks original."

"I want an explanation—now!" Clare demanded.

"Okay, Mom, okay."

CHAPTER 16

the grass needs cutting

SHE WOULD NOT let him keep it. A bike from a stranger, a stranger Clare had never met and Jeremy had never mentioned. Jeremy tried to explain but she would have none of it. He promised he would return the bicycle, but like all good teenage lawyers he didn't give a date or time. A promise he would keep "henceforth" on a day of his choosing. In word and action he misled his mother as he pushed off from the curb, with her watching suspiciously from the stoop, her distrust realized as Jeremy headed toward the bay and not toward school and Roy's farm to return the bicycle as he had promised.

"That's the wrong way!" she shouted. Jeremy realized the error of his deception, turned around, smiled at Clare, and headed in the direction of school only to turn again after she walked back down into the dark belly of their basement apartment.

He was all smiles riding the Schwinn with a pocketful of money toward the ferry. *It rides as good as it looks!* The large tires, sturdy frame, and the weight of the bike connected him to the road like his modern-day, high-tech bicycle simply couldn't. He sat taller and more upright, both the bicycle and road speaking to him through the springs connected to the bottom of the comfortable leather seat.

Autocycle. Rides like a car but it's a bicycle. I can't give this thing up. What a ride! Bike speed? This thing must fly. As he pushed toward bike speed his mind raced, wondering how he could keep it. Clare gave him a handful of reasons on why he had to return the bike, all of which made sense. But her reasoning gave way to his senses as he opened the bike up, the breeze of speed freeing him from the confines of adult rule.

"Yes!" he shouted. "Bike speed! Freedom!"

Jeremy approached the dock, basking in the familiar warmth of the sun, the salted sea air filling his lungs. The tranquility of the water always put a smile on his face, even on the most uncertain of days.

The ferry *Stranger* groaned uncomfortably as it pressed against the large wooden pier, awaiting passengers and cargo, its crewmembers busily preparing for the thirty-minute, nine-mile journey. It looked like a half a world away from Jeremy's castle in the sand, and he stared at it for what seemed a lifetime.

Jeremy noticed the line of ticketed passengers. They were campers, bikers, fishermen, beachgoers, rowdy college students, gay lovers, and families of every stripe. Jeremy was none of the above, but noticed the one thing common to them all—their smiles and laughter.

He was alone in the crowd, alone among the smiling, the weight of his journey expressed in a tightened chest and frenetic mind as he approached the ticket office. The others had come to fish, to bathe, to swim, to drink, to eat, to sail, to camp, or just simply to see this magical place where the grind of life bore down a bit lighter if only for a short visit.

Jeremy had come to see where the promise was made. To go to the place where his mom had fallen in love with his father, to touch the sand, smell the sea, walk the long trails. The place, as his mother had so said, "Where a wooden trail leads to a bench facing the ocean, where seagulls dance against blue sky and the world promised it was going to be all right." What he was to discover he was unable to express in words or image, but something inside him urged him to press on. Something pressed him to go, and something pressed him to run away.

Passengers started boarding as the *Stranger* blew its air horn. "Last call for the two-thirty to Davis Park, Fire Island!" the man behind the counter shouted.

It's time. It's time. Jeremy pulled out his pocketful of money and walked toward the counter. Do you know who you are? And who you are meant to become? Most dare not ask, dare not take the journey, and dare not be naked to the truth of oneself. Jeremy knew that his life could change, but he had to change first. Fear filled his lungs; doubt clouded his mind. The *Stranger's* air horn filled the air, screaming of its departure and his call to arms, to charge forward not with sword in hand to slay demons, vampires, and goblins but to charge forward and find that unknown place within, that better place he'd yet to inhabit.

Charge, damn it! Charge! Heed the call! He was too comfortable in his anger, too content in his indifference, but what was he to become without it? He had pressed to make sense of this world and his place in it, but the world does not reveal itself to the timid, to those who do not dare, to those who do not dream.

The ropes unslung, the walkway removed, the *Stranger* pulled away, bellowing a scream like a dying animal. Jeremy sheathed his sword, pocketed his money, and anxiously bicycled away from the pier.

◆　◆　◆

Routine is essential for a patient suffering from Alzheimer's. It's familiar to the healthy and essential to the sick. Sarah's decline had steepened, and Roy felt he needed to do more. The routine and surroundings of the nursing home were no longer mooring her to reality. Desperate, he knew the farm was home, the best medicine, like their ocean walks, like the songs they sang together.

He had an ally. A new doctor had arrived from Florida with a novel way of thinking about the disease. Dr. R. didn't believe in pumping patients full of experimental drugs or drugs of limited effectiveness. Healthy organic food along with talk therapy evoking memories of the past could help anchor patients to the reality of the present. If memories could be stirred by music, singing, gardening, painting, or something as simple as a massage, it should be done. It was far healthier and more humane than the expensive, druggy treatments pushed by conventional medicine. A chocolate ice cream soda topped with whipped cream and maraschino cherries—Sarah's lifelong favorite dessert—always put her in better spirits. It engaged her in the present-day like no drug from Merck or Pfizer.

On those days when nothing but the farm would settle her anxiety and fear, Dr. R. gave permission to take her home for the day. The nursing home's lawyer protested, citing their liability if she were injured, even threatening Dr. R.'s job. Undeterred, the doctor believed the dictates of caretaking took precedent over the nursing home lawyer's pecuniary priggishness. His response was succinct: "If I didn't it would be malpractice, and that would cost you a hell of a lot more than the six thousand dollars a month you overcharge her for being here."

But even with all the care and all the love, Dr. R., Roy, and perhaps even Sarah herself knew the end was near. The river of her consciousness that once flowed mightily had ebbed to a trickle. She spoke infrequently, and only then with a few words or a short phrase. She began to wander and not respond to her surroundings.

Jeremy rolled up to the hay barn, his ride from the pier unsettling. The day, filled with apprehension but also hope, was not going according to plan. The television show where he learned the word "henceforth" and was therefore able to misconstrue it for his personal gain was precise in language as numbers were to math. He would return the bike. Henceforth, today, now, from this time forth. *Damn.*

Jeremy looked out over the field and there he saw Roy standing a few feet behind Sarah. Roy followed her as she walked the open expanse of the field. Roy watched carefully, hoping home would awaken a memory, and a memory a response. Nothing. Roy waved Jeremy over, who then rode the bicycle to the middle of the field.

"Nice ride," Roy said.

"Yes, it is. Thank you, Mr. Roy."

"I figured you needed one."

"I do, but my mom said to return it. Said it ain't right taking gifts from strangers. Ain't right she gets free money from the government, but I can't have this bike."

Jeremy and Roy watched Sarah as she walked slowly but deliberately, her eyes closed and face tilted skyward to the autumn sun.

"I'm sure your mom is doing the best she can. You tell her I have no use for it," said Roy. "Not at my age."

"I did."

"Sarah. Sarah, this is Jeremy," Roy said. She didn't respond nor turn around. Jeremy took in Roy's expression, not one of embarrassment but utter sadness. He didn't know what was wrong and dared not ask.

"I guess I can just keep the bike and not tell her."

"Now that's not right."

"I know, but I want the bike," Jeremy said. *Screw henceforth. I want the bike. Why not?* Jeremy looked around at the knee-high grass. He'd never operated a lawnmower. The many rented apartments he'd lived in were always surrounded by untended dirt and weeds.

"Grass is getting pretty long. You sure I can't earn the bike by cutting the grass? My mom might agree to that."

"We back to that? Bush-hog, cut the grass, with my tractor?"

"I was figuring a lawnmower."

"A lawnmower?" Roy repeated, incredulous. "Look around, son. It would take you two weeks with a mower. Just keep the bike and don't tell her."

"You just said that wasn't right." Jeremy said.

"At my age I'm allowed to contradict myself."

"Why can't you just let—"

"Cause no one drives my tractor except me. And two, it's over sixty years old and couldn't take a newbie grinding the gears, over-torqueing the transmission, overheating the engine. No thanks."

"You can spend more time with your wife. You can walk on the beach, hold hands, and sing to her?"

There was a long silence.

"Those days are over," Roy mumbled.

"My mom used to sing to me. She doesn't sing anymore."

"Why not?"

"I drive her crazy."

Roy snorted. "I can see that."

"I think it's just life—I guess it gets the best of us."

"That it does, son. That it does."

"The gra . . . ss . . . ne . . . eds cut. Cut . . . ting," Sarah slurred. Roy and Jeremy looked at her. She was facing them, her eyes still closed, her face still skyward, bathing in the warm fall sun.

"Sarah. Sarah!" Roy said.

"The grass ne . . . eds cut . . . ting," Sarah repeated.

"Yes, yes, yes it does," Roy said with a large smile, his face flushed with joy. It wasn't much, but to him it was the world. He'd heard those words for fifty-plus years, sometimes begrudgingly. This time it never sounded so good.

"The grass needs cut . . . ting," she said again.

"Yes, it does, sweetie. Yes, it does," Roy said. Sarah opened her eyes, looked at Roy and then at Jeremy.

"The bo . . . y, Roy. Let the boy cu . . . t the gra . . . ss. Trac . . . tor. Tea . . . ch him," she said with a smile. And the river flowed, if just for a few moments, bringing joy to Roy that would carry him for another day.

CHAPTER 17

neither here nor there

MOST OF THE KIDS at Frontier were part of the national school lunch program. The food left a lot to be desired for anyone with taste buds. Fed empty calories and little nutrition, Jeremy was always a slight bit hungry, and he would never have believed that a girl could equal his own voracious appetite, but Kelli certainly did. His Fire Island expedition a failure, he wanted to talk to her, needed to talk to her, and figured himself willing to pay for the privilege.

Kelli sat alone on the grass leaning against the razor-wire perimeter fence licking the grease from the empty french fry container as Jeremy walked over.

"I bought you a second lunch," Jeremy said.

"What'd that cost you?" Kelli asked.

"How 'bout none of your business and thank you."

"Nothing's free. What's up?"

"After I first met you, I had a dream. You were in it."

"Oh, Lord. I'm not going to have sex—"

"It wasn't that type of dream! I didn't want to tell you," Jeremy said as he handed her the box lunch.

"Burger?" she asked.

"Yep, with cheese."

"Nice. Fries?"

"No, salad."

"Mistake. I don't like anything green."

"It's good for you," he said.

"Ice cream sandwich?"

"Yes."

"Excellent. That's nice of you, Jeremy. Thanks. What's up?"

"Why haven't you been talking to me?"

"If you haven't noticed, I'm doing my work. What was your dream about? And why are you telling me now?"

"I'll get to it. I can't relate to anything. I don't understand why I have to learn about American history or sea shells or rocks. They don't interest me."

"What does?"

"Not much."

"English?"

"I already know how to talk," he said.

"You're nicer than I thought but also dumber than I thought."

"Thanks."

"You're welcome. Read?" she asked.

"Cereal box in the morning."

"That's a start. You do realize everything here is reading on the computer."

"I do."

"Don't expect Mr. Collins to teach you."

"I'm not that dumb. I can read—"

"I don't doubt that," she interrupted. "But to really read, to learn—that takes focus."

"I'm not interested—"

"Nope. It's focus. And if you can't focus you can't read and if you can't read you're just wasting your time here."

Everything at Frontier was done on the computers bolted to the students' desks. One hundred and sixty self-paced modules from English to science followed by a twenty-five question multiple-choice test at the end of each lesson. If you passed, it registered a pleasant "bleep" with the teacher's computer and you were on to the next module, one step closer to graduation. If you failed, Mr. Collins's computer bleeped in an unpleasant tone, interrupting his reading of the *Times* or worse, waking him from his midday nap. He'd look up with contempt, say a few choice words, and on a good day just yell out the correct answers. He'd reset the test and you'd try again. On bad days he'd walk over to your desk and, along with the ridicule and the waft of cheap cologne, coffee breath, and the stale, fetid, vinegary smell of his sweat, actually make a sincere attempt to teach.

"I suppose you don't need to know about math?" Kelli asked.

"I know how to add, subtract, and multiply. Division gives me problems."

"It gives everyone problems. One day you'll need to know how to divide. It might get you a job."

"Computers can do that for you."

"Not the one on your desk. And that's the only one that counts, Last Third."

"Please don't call me that."

"Your nickname is Division. You're divided. Get it?"

"Cute."

"I see it. Do you?" she asked. He was silent. "Jeremy, I like social studies more than science. I found out you don't have to like everything. I sure don't, but I've found the subjects I liked 'cause we've been introduced to them at school. I want to teach. Social studies."

"Why?"

"To know the past or at least to try to understand the past, and with that—"

"The future. Blah, blah, blah."

"Now you're annoying me, and that's hard to do," she said.

"Okay. Sorry. So what do I do?"

"You'll have to find the answer to that on your own. Your dream. Tell me—"

"I don't know where to—"

"From the beginning," she said. He didn't answer and sat looking at her in silence.

"Why are you staring at my hands?"

"I'm not."

"Yes, you are. From the beginning."

At first he spoke haltingly and in a low voice, as if he wasn't deserving of speaking about himself. She listened, and slowly his confidence projected in voice and manner. And for the first time in his young life he shared of himself like he had never done before. And in midsentence, midthought, the realization came to him. He heard the *Stranger's* bellow, and it made him want to charge forward, sword in hand, and find that better place he'd yet to inhabit. *Fly or fall. Find your way tonight. Maybe she could go with me. Help me get on that ferry.* Partial courage is the stuff of goblins and vampires, the stuff of fantasy, neither here nor there, not worthy of the revelation of dream. He didn't ask but desperately wanted to. The taste of partial courage. The taste of mac and cheese. Cold.

At thought's end he fell silent waiting for a response, begging for one. But Kelli said nothing.

The bell rang. Kelli stood and looked at him for a few seconds as he looked at the ground beneath him. She ran the outside of her hand gently against the side of his face, the way only a mother could do, and walked toward class.

"Almost," Jeremy mumbled under his breath. "Almost."

CHAPTER 18

bridge way house

ANOTHER FITFUL NIGHT brought Jeremy hours of racing thoughts and little sleep. As the sun rose he made a promise to himself and went to school with a plan. This time he'd find the courage to ask Kelli to go to Fire Island with him. But she wasn't there. It was as if to spite him, his emotions getting the best of him, but he knew that not to be the case. By being absent, her presence felt even greater.

Her seat empty, his mind filled with their past conversations and the soft touch of her hand. *I can do this!* He entered his password: LASTTHIRD3. Jeremy began reading:

Science Module Two: Mollusks.

Mollusks . . .

I can do this.

Jeremy was drawn to Kelli's desk.

You see I can *do this.*

He read:

A mollusk has an outer shell, a soft body, and a muscular foot that it uses for movement. It has a heart, blood, and blood vessels. Snails and clams are mollusks. Octopuses and squid are also mollusks . . .

"How can that be?" he mumbled.

In this module we'll explore the range of species called mollusks . . .

How can that be? A clam and a squid are the same? How can that be? How can two things so different be called the same thing?

Jeremy looked around the room. *We aren't all the same. I see troublemakers, juvenile delinquents, bullies! Clams and octopuses are different! Who says we're all the same? I'm not like these people! She's not like these people.*

"What are you looking at, convict?" Collins asked. He put down the Style section of the *New York Times* and walked over to Kelli's desk, pulled the seat out, and sat facing Jeremy.

"Well?" he asked.

"Well, nothing. I didn't ask for your help."

"What's bothering you? Not that I care, but Dirty Harry over there looks like he's itching for a fight." Both looked over at the security guard sitting uneasily in the corner of the room. "What's your problem?"

"Mollusks," Jeremy said.

"Mollusks? Shellfish? That's what got you agitated? Bottom feeders? Okay, I'll play. What about them?"

"How can a squid and a clam be considered the same thing?"

"They're shellfish," Collins replied.

"I've never seen a squid with a shell."

"They're a subgroup in the shellfish category."

"They should be called something different."

Collins smirked. "I'm sure they don't mind. A dolphin is a mammal and so is a human. Get it?"

"No, I don't."

"Humans and dolphins have common traits. Warm-blooded, a four-chambered heart, the females produce milk and nurture their young for many years," Collins said, remembering his days of teaching biology. He wondered how long it had been since he had actually taught a full class period on any subject.

"Nurture their young—how do they know that?"

"Scientific observation. There's a saying in the teaching profession: if you've met the child, you've met the parent. And yes, it's something your mother knows nothing about."

Jeremy angrily rose from his seat and stood nose to nose with Collins, who waved at the security guard to keep his distance without looking over.

"Sit down or you'll end up in Albany," Collins said in a low, dangerous voice. "Where you should have been in the first place. Son, what's your game?"

Jeremy didn't answer.

"Sit down if you know what's good for you. Which you obviously don't, as you haven't done a damn thing since you've gotten here."

"I'm trying!" Jeremy yelled.

"Try harder or else!"

"Else what?!"

"You'll find out soon enough. Now get back to whatever you were doing."

Jeremy sat and tried to calm himself. His mind wandered. Like the gravitational effect of the moon on the ocean tides, his thoughts pulled him to his castle by the sea and suddenly back to her. He looked toward Kelli's desk and could see the curve of her ear, the bend of her belly, but it was the pure joy of learning, her wide grin that followed, and her simple wisdom he remembered most. *How does she do it?* He thought about the beauty of the setting sun coloring the bay in an orange hue and was calmed. Thoughts of her simply couldn't be swept to sea by the tides of his thoughts. Nor did he want them to.

The cursor on the computer vanished and the login page reappeared; it had timed out. Her compass could navigate to the far horizon, to his ship, rudderless and without bearing. *She can get me there.*

Jeremy had no intention of sitting idly in class, his mind a chaotic mess. He escaped during lunch hour and asked one of the bus drivers for the address to the Bridge Way House. Tomorrow couldn't wait.

The six-mile bike ride to Bridge Way House unearthed many questions, and by ride's end her words abounded in his head.

Jeremy was surprised to find Bridge Way House at the end of an old residential neighborhood. The house was obscured from the street, large trees and shrubs providing a living wall of privacy. On a sprawling piece of land adjacent to the bay it had multiple chimneys, weathered brick, copper awnings, and gas lanterns that harkened back to a more gilded age. The mansion was as nature is. Living. Real. Not a speck of plastic or faux brick, because old money is cedar and oak and maple, not vinyl siding.

He looked but couldn't find a sign on the front of the house as if it were a business advertising itself, just the street number etched into a large stone by the curb. Jeremy read the number to confirm that this was the place. He rode his bicycle down the large driveway to the front door of the house, a house he believed to be older than his bicycle. *This definitely ain't no shelter.*

Jeremy lifted the iron doorknob from the arched wooden entrance and looked curiously at the detailed carvings in the dark wooden door as the knocker made a loud thump. An elderly woman with silver hair and an elegant manner answered. She looked like a throwback to the golden era of Hollywood, a starlet on one of those black-and-white movies he'd flipped past on the TV's classic channel. But the shade of her skin was as different as his. Jeremy's nervousness was lessened by her genteel voice and warm smile. "Hello, young man. How are you today?" she asked.

"I'm fine, thanks. Is Kelli here? I don't know her last name. She goes to Frontier."

"Yes, Kelli. We call her 'Red.' Lovely young lady. And your name?"

"Jeremy."

"Carol."

"Hello, Mrs. Carol. Is she sick today?"

"Jeremy, may I ask the reason for your visit?"

"Life," he said.

"Life? Whose?"

"Mine."

"Oh, dear. And what about your life?"

"I don't exactly know but I think she does."

"Well then," Carol answered after a long pause. "Who's a lady of my age to question a young man coming all this way to my home—on a bicycle, by the way, that I remember from my years as a young child—asking the biggest of questions? And who better than a mother-to-be to answer them? Come with me, young man. Where did you get such a treasure as that bike?"

"An old man ran me over with his tractor and felt bad about it so he gave it to me."

"Tractor?"

"Yeah, a tractor," Jeremy said with pride.

"Tractor trail—"

"Farm tractor. My mom asked that too."

Jeremy followed Carol through the large arched doors and into the foyer of the home. His mind raced as he entered, not knowing what to expect of a house filled with pregnant girls.

The interior was as grand as the exterior, with stone floors, exposed beams, and aged tapestries hanging from the twenty-foot stucco walls. Light from the afternoon sun passed through the towering bands of stained-glass windows that stretched from the vaulted ceiling above to the stone floor covered in ornate rugs below. The rainbow of light highlighted the stone fireplace that was as big as a truck. Taken by the room's beauty and warmth and Carol's hospitality, Jeremy's anxiety lessened even more.

"It's usually never this quiet," she said.

"Where are all the—"

"Babies?" Carol asked, then surprised Jeremy with her operatic laugh. "The babies are in the daycare center on the other side of the house. The girls are in school, just like you should be." She pointed to the veranda, where Kelli sat in the shade of the covered terrace looking over the Great South Bay.

"She's a bit under the weather, but I think she could use the company," Carol said.

Jeremy stepped onto the terrace to see Kelli sitting comfortably in an Adirondack chair, covered in blankets with her feet elevated on throw pillows. Her skin pale and eyes sunken, it looked as if she was in deep thought after surviving some natural disaster. On the large wooden armrest lay soda crackers, small slices of watermelon, and water, all apparently untouched.

"Jeremy!" Kelli said, shedding her exhausted state if only for a moment.

"Kelli, I hope you don't—"

"Stalker!" she laughed. "First a convict, now a stalker! Welcome!"

"This place is beautiful."

"I know. If you want in just get pregnant and get kicked out of your house."

"Getting kicked out, I think I could manage."

"I know what brings you here."

"I'd like—"

"Help."

"Would you—"

"Of course."

"Can I finish a sentence?!" he snapped.

"Sorry. Gift of the witches."

"No problem. I'd—"

"The guilt, the anger. Free yourself of it. Talk to your mother. Tell her how you feel," she said.

"This is not about my mom! It's about—"

"You've never read Shakespeare," she interrupted again. "It's always about—"

"Can I finish—"

"Nope! I'll finish *my* sentences too, not just yours. *Family.* And you are part of one. Father, mother, son. You're as clueless about your life as how you got here!"

"I rode my bike."

"Don't be a dick!"

"And *your* family?" he said.

"They know where I am and I've invited them here," she said.

"Fuck them, then!"

"Nope. It's their right. Now say it for me. Why are you here?"

"Because."

"Because why! Family! Say it, Jeremy! Say it!"

"No!"

"Say it! Family! It's not perfect but it's all we got! Semen, egg, gestation, newborn! You think that's family? It's not! That's biology. To hell with those who judge me! Who judge you! The looks, the scorn, the ridicule, that's easy." Kelli pointed to her vagina. "When my baby comes out, that's when it's going to be tough! And that's when the real shit begins!" She regarded him with an angry look. "Your mother loves you, you know."

"How would you know? You've never met her!"

"And that's why you're here. I remind you of her!"

"Yuck!" he said.

"What do you mean, yuck?"

"I don't like my mother the way I like you."

"Yuck!" she said. "For Christ sakes, you like me that way? Shit!"

"I'll leave."

"No, no, no. Ask me and I'll say yes."

"Ask you what?"

"God, men really are dumb! About why you came here!"

"I need you to go somewhere with me."

"Good," she said with relief. "Ask me and I'll say yes."

"You will?"

"Sure, why wouldn't I?"

"But you don't even know where."

"Fine, tell me."

"Fire Island," he said.

"Okay."

"But you don't know why."

"Wrong. Father. Like you wanted to tell me yesterday."

"My God you are—"

"Yep. Pregnant woman. Special vaginal powers! Super powers!" Kelli raised her arms and flexed her muscles.

"You knew yesterday."

"I sensed something—"

"Why didn't—"

"Because it has to come from you, Jeremy. Want some watermelon?"

"You want to know why we're going there?"

"You can tell me on the ferry while I'm throwing up. I hate boats."

"Thanks."

"I used to love watermelon," Kelli said.

"What happened?"

"Ask my hormones. Women stuff."

"You don't look well."

"Neither would you if you'd been throwing up all day. Your mom went through this, you know. She didn't give you up. That counts for something, doesn't it?"

Jeremy looked out upon the bay and Fire Island in the distance. Kelli got up from the Adirondack chair and stood beside him.

"This weekend," she said. "I should be good by then."

"If not—"

"I'll take my chances. Follow me."

"Where we going?" he asked.

"We're going to look back in time. A mirror of sorts." Kelli led Jeremy through the large Tudor mansion to the west side of the house. As they approached they could hear the sounds of babies crying.

"I don't need to go in there," he said.

"Yes, you do." Kelli opened the hallway door to a large room for babies, children, and a host of child-care providers. Babies cried and Jeremy wondered if their howl was for their missing fathers. Carol, holding a crying newborn, welcomed Jeremy as the baby, barely able to focus, locked in on Jeremy and quieted.

His eyes fixed on the baby, he watched as the small fingers wiggled and clasped at the air as if to grab it. *Does this baby dream? Did I dream as a baby?* He saw his reflection in the baby's large blue eyes. His face flushed, his mind traveled back as far as memory permitted, and there at memory's edge all he could do was imagine. No guilt, no unending sadness, no abandonment. This was no dream.

CHAPTER 19

math

THREE, TWO, ONE. Jeremy watched as the minute hand of the school clock struck 3 p.m. and bolted out the door before the bell fell silent. The same beginning as his normal routine, but this day was different—he had somewhere to go, a place to be, an appointment with the old man.

Bike speed would lead to tractor speed and another first for Jeremy: employment of sorts.

"Six gears?" Jeremy asked. He sat atop the American Harvester as Roy explained the machine that enveloped the enthusiastic teenager.

"Yeah, that's right, and if I see you in any but the first three you'll never captain this ship again," Roy said. "Understood?"

"Understood."

Tractor speed was fine with Jeremy. Roy had been hesitant at first, but he'd made a promise to his wife and he would keep it. Gus was the only non-Higgins to have ever bush-hogged the farm, helping during the war years when Roy was fighting in the Pacific. Now a lifetime later Roy heard his father's echo with every instruction he barked at the young boy.

"Slow and in control," he said. "It's not like a bike or a car.

Speed gets you in trouble. You don't run a bull—it runs you, at least this one."

Jeremy sat atop the five-thousand-pound steel harvester, knowing nothing about clutches, parking brakes, or the myriad of levers and pedals before him. He counted six excluding the steering wheel and smiled when Roy turned the key and the forty-horsepower engine kicked over, spewing diesel exhaust and shaking his body toe to head.

"A good ole reliable tractor will last forever if you take care of it," Roy said.

"Nothing lasts forever," Jeremy said.

"You're right, son. The best we can do is a long time."

"How old is this thing?"

"Almost as old as me."

"That's old."

"Yes it is, wiseass. She's listening."

"Who?"

"Her," Roy said over the rumble of the engine as he pointed to the tractor. "Now listen carefully!" He pointed to the clutch pedal. "Hold it down."

Jeremy watched as Roy, standing on the foot step and holding on to the side of the tractor, put it in first gear.

"Now slowly ease up on the clutch," Roy said. Ease is a relative term, and as with everything in Jeremy's life nothing was easy, except that clutch. He let up too quickly and the tractor bucked, throwing Jeremy off the back end as quickly as he'd climbed on. The engine chugged, spewed, and finally quit in protest, and Jeremy lay splayed once again on the grass behind it.

"Son of a b—" Jeremy said.

"I said slowly! Now get back on; we'll try again."

"Again?"

"Again!"

"Again," Jeremy said with conviction. He climbed back on the tractor, now understanding "slowly" in practical terms. As Roy had been taught by his father, he would start with the clutch before working his way to the brakes and throttle. Over the period of a few hours Roy would teach Jeremy how each lever, pedal, and switch was used to tame the bull and cut the grass.

At first unfamiliar and uninviting, the tractor required both feet and hands working individually and at times in concert, and Roy wondered if the aging tractor could endure the brute touch of a newbie. Jeremy eagerly listened to Roy's instruction, his enthusiasm undeterred even after a few more bucks from the bull.

Jeremy quickly learned that tractor and boy was not a relationship of equals. The machine dictates. It demands. It simply doesn't ask. If you don't listen or understand you end up on your ass in the grass. If function was the constant, "feel" was the variable. It took more than patience; it required Jeremy to listen. But to what?

"Maybe if you taught me what all these damn numbers mean, I wouldn't get bucked off this bull!" Jeremy protested.

"Those gauges—'damn numbers' as you call them—will tell you what your body already knows," Roy said.

"Well—"

"Well, nothing! Listen to what the tractor's telling you. You don't drive a tractor watching the oil temperature or RPM gauge!"

"How then?"

"With your ears, with your hands, with your feet, with your butt, with the machine talking to you through your body."

"Butt?"

"Yep, your butt. Seat of your pants. Flying expression. Largest part of your body in contact with the tractor. Let it talk to you. Listen!"

"And the gauges?" Jeremy asked.

"They'll back up what your ears, hands, and butt tell you about how fast the engine is running. The sound of it. The vibration of the transmission. The push of the wheels. The pull of the cutter. All through your body. The gauges back up what your body already knows. That's math, son. The gauges give you the math of what the tractor is telling you through your senses."

"But—"

"But nothing. Listen!" Roy said. And Jeremy did. It took a while, but he did. With every mistake, a lesson learned and an error corrected, the inventory of first-hand experience accumulated and he learned to trust . . . himself, to listen, to understand and develop a tentative trust with the machine. And as Roy said, the gauges told him what the tractor was telling him through his senses.

It was as promised, as neat and clean as a math problem. Every control on the tractor had a specific function. Every number had a specific value. Combine the value of two numbers, combine the function of two controls, and you have something of exponential value. The numbers had greater value, the lever, pedal, and switches had greater purpose, and the grass stood no chance. Jeremy marveled at the creators of the machine.

And for the first time he "understood" math when he listened to the muse of a sixty-year-old tractor.

Roy watched as the kid's grip on the steering wheel lightened, his feet were no longer a vise on the pedals, his heels slid to the floorboard, and his posture on the seat was more upright and relaxed. He needed to understand form and function to be free of it, and when he did he became one with the machine.

"This is on fleek!" Jeremy yelled. "Better than bike speed!" After a long first day, bruised not by bicycle or skateboard, not by bully or the brutal dictates of life, he looked out on all he'd accomplished. The rows of cut grass were uneven, the lines crooked, and he'd even missed a few spots, but they were his and his only. His face softened, his smile turned to a grin, and the sweet scent of cut grass filled his lungs.

"Feels good, doesn't it?" Roy said. "Looks more like Picasso than Norman Rockwell, but that's all right. Damn good for the first day. Now a few more lines and let's put her to bed. You're on your own, kid."

"You're not going to help me anymore?" Jeremy asked.

"Three's a crowd. Just you and the bull now." Roy smiled and stepped off the tractor's footrest and onto the cut grass. He watched as the tractor drove on without him, knowing every bump and turn that Jeremy was experiencing. He watched with pride but also a shameful envy, reaching out with his outstretched arm and open hand as if to say, "Wait! Come back!"

You're right, son, he thought. *The best we can do is a long time. Nothing lasts forever except the earth and sky.*

This sacred place he tilled and toiled. This place a monument to a life well lived. This place of a lifetime shared was coming to an end. And it was . . . all right.

Roy walked toward the farmhouse and sat on the porch as his father had done the very first time he'd driven the tractor. He listened to the rhythmic purr of the diesel engine, watched the cut of the blades throw the coarse grass into the air, and observed the obedient trail of the tractor's exhaust. Jeremy threw him a wave and a smile.

That's why I fly, he thought. *It was that smile, that joy knowing you'd never catch the setting sun but would sure have fun trying.*

He'd make a fine aviator. Farm kids usually do.

CHAPTER 20

jeter jump throw

JEREMY OPENED THE FIRST math module, his curiosity heightened after his tractor lesson the previous day, though the problems on the computer screen were still exercises in the abstract. He was trying, trying to . . . relate, to perform calculations that, to him, had no significance but to determine whether you followed the formula and landed on the correct answer. An answer he couldn't confirm through the timbre of his ears nor the vibration in his hands or body. How he wished Kelli was there to see it. The cursor moved. Despite her absence he continued, and every correct answer was a small but surprising victory, a small battle won, a reprieve from a mind wandering aimlessly day after day.

He smiled with every math problem answered, his interest in the subject rising. With every correct answer, another mystery solved. Learning math became something he never thought possible: fun. And for the first time since his arrival at Frontier he completed a module, and with a score of 100 percent at that. It registered at Mr. Collins's desk, and he looked up with suspicion to see Jeremy smiling.

Jeremy completed two more math lessons before his mind lapsed back to its wandering. It was his best day at Frontier. A beginning.

The school day over, Jeremy biked toward Roy's farm. His racing mind was filled with numbers. He'd never played this game before, his consciousness heretofore a rudderless ship wandering a vast ocean of nothingness, math not part of the horizon or any part of the equation. To his surprise he started to see math in the everyday. He saw the sun's position in the sky and he "knew" it was 3 p.m. His hamstrings and calves heated up, their muscle memory signaling to his brain that he was two miles from the farm. His brow cooled and his body knew that it was around sixty degrees. *Three percent, three meters, three milligrams. Fractions, 1/3, 2/3, 3/3. Three divided by three is one. First third, second third, last third.*

"Last third!" Jeremy shouted as he biked toward the farm.

◆ ◆ ◆

Jeremy walked clockwise around the Stearman, looking at it closely as if he were seeing it for the first time, sizing it up as closely as the police officer checking him before entering school. It was as foreign to him as anything he'd ever known. Airplanes were "over there," a thing to be read about, to be seen from a distance; flying them was what others did in dreams or life. *Me? Me. Me!* He dared to imagine.

He pressed his index finger against the yellow wing. It was taut yet soft to the touch, and he was surprised to discover that it was painted fabric. The fuselage was thin metal and also gave with a hint of pressure. *How can this be?* The Stearman looked gangly, like a sleeping giraffe splayed on the soft grass. Legs, arms, and neck strewn everywhere. *Do giraffes sleep lying down?* He ran his hand the length of the wooden propeller, its leading edge of forged metal, and he wondered if it was made from the forest in his midst.

The bulky engine warmed by the afternoon sun felt heavy on the hand. It offered a drop of oil that Jeremy rolled between his fingers.

He knew the fury of this engine and didn't know what to make of its silence. The only sound was the distant chime of a church bell welcoming the new hour. The oil had a slight airy scent and the same greasy consistency of the french fries served at school.

The smell evoked a memory of the cafeteria clan. *How's Big Mac doing?* It wasn't that he cared—he didn't. After the beating the police officers had forced him to look at the photos of Big Mac's pummeled face. He'd been unimpressed. *If they only knew.* His only outward emotions were tears when Clare was permitted to see him after he'd been locked up for two days. It was a fear deep within him, something he'd never expressed, the fear of losing his mom. He apologized to her not for the vicious act of violence but for the burden he'd been since birth and the uncertainty of the road he was about to embark.

But in that act of self-preservation, as violent as it was, and as contradictory to the tenets of peace and the rule of law, it had brought him to this place. And in the greatest of ironies life was looking up. At least for now.

Jeremy peered inquisitively into the open cockpit of the Stearman as if inspecting a rotting giraffe carcass on the subtropical plains of Africa. It was larger than he imagined, with long metal tubing pressing against the thin yellow skin, reminding him of the skeleton of some prehistoric creature he'd seen on a school trip to the Museum of Natural History. He dared not get in, but this is what he had come to see— the inside, the controls, the things that commanded this beast. The math of it all.

What he saw was the complexity of the tractor tenfold. Numbers on stacks of round gauges. Gauges within gauges, dials within dials, and all pointing at numbers, numbers that must mean something though he did not know what. Numbers that no teacher, principal, nor parent needed tell of their importance. There was one gauge he could decipher—a clock—and he smiled knowing he had read one of the instruments. It was time. Four o'clock. He knew little to nothing about the others scribed on the gauges—RPM, temperature °C, knots, altitude, oil, climb (up-down)—but he was curious.

He saw metal tubes, wire cables, large foot pedals, and levers of different colors and shapes and wondered of their purpose, their function. At the center standing alone among the cacophony of stuff was the control stick, the yoke. It rose slightly above the seat from the floor of scuffed sheet metal and wood. Its design was simple among the complexity of its surroundings.

Jeremy eyed the seat. He'd never much thought about flying. *You sit when you fly.* He'd seen the early photos of Orville and Wilbur Wright lying prone while flying their glider. *Just like Superman, just like in my dreams. But this is no dream, this isn't make believe. No superheroes, vampires, or sorcerers with English accents.* Again, he looked at the seat. He was familiar with . . . sitting. He chuckled. A lifetime of sitting. Sitting in the cold metal seat at the Fifth Precinct being questioned by two detectives, the high chair being fed Cheerios as a baby, the seat at school, his leather bicycle seat, the couch his mother occupied watching daytime television, the kitchen chair eating macaroni and cheese, the toilet. Shitting. Sitting.

"Grass don't grow back in one day."

Jeremy turned around to see Roy. "I know how you are with the tractor. Don't like people using your stuff."

"You're getting smarter by the day. What's up?"

"I was curious," Jeremy said. "After you teaching me how to drive the tractor, I was wondering about—"

"What do you see in there?"

"Looks like a mess to me."

"Me too, the first time. What do you see?" Roy asked.

"Lots of dials, gauges, numbers."

"And?"

"And what?"

"What do they give you? Remember what I told you about the tractor?"

"Yeah," Jeremy said. "Listen to the tractor and it will tell you what you need to know, what you need to do. The gauges will back that up."

"That's right. I can fly this thing with all those gauges covered up."

"Really? Then why are they there?"

"That's a good question. When someone learns to dance they look at their feet. When you learn how to play guitar you look at the strings, your hands, the frets on the neck of the guitar. But once you've learned—"

"You don't need to."

"No, you need to, but not as much," Roy said. "So I ask you again, what do you see in there?"

Jeremy was silent. His mind raced for an intelligent response.

"Information," Roy said.

"Looks like too much info to me."

"You read a novel one word at a time, don't ya?"

"Guess so. I don't read novels."

"Then start."

"I've been told that before," Jeremy said.

"With time it's similar to driving the tractor. Takes a lot more time though."

"Wow. Cool shit."

"That it is. You never did get to Fire Island, did you?"

"How did you know?"

"Son, at my age you just know things. That's called wisdom. How 'bout that low pass?"

"Now?"

"Why not, perfect afternoon for a flight."

"Really?" Jeremy asked in disbelief.

"No shit, Socrates. Follow me."

Jeremy hesitated. "Are you sure?"

"You wanna go?" Roy asked.

"Yeah!"

"Then listen and learn. Seven turns of the propeller. Why seven?"

Jeremy followed Roy to the front of the Stearman. "You gonna start this thing?"

"You going to answer my question?" Roy asked.

"Okay. Why seven?"

"Good question. Everything you do when you fly has a purpose. Count the cylinders."

"Seven."

"Correct. Gotta stretch before you run—the plane, that is. I'll turn the propeller seven turns; it cycles the oil and clears each cylinder of any vapor." Roy reached for the prop and turned it ninety degrees. Jeremy took a step back, expecting the engine and propeller to come to life, but with each turn the engine let out a wheeze.

"Sounds like it's farting," Roy said. "What you're hearing is the fuel vapor being released through the exhaust."

Jeremy smiled in wonder as Roy walked to the left side of the Stearman just behind the engine. "What's that?"

"To start the engine it needs fuel," Roy said. "It's a primer."

"A what?"

"It's a shot of gas directly into the engine." Roy unfastened the safety clip and drew the cylindrical metal syringe outward, away from the flush skin of the fuselage. "You hear the gas filling the tube?"

"Yeah, that's pretty cool."

"Now press it back in," Roy said. Jeremy pushed on the metal tube. At first it resisted, but with increased pressure he could feel and hear the gas entering the engine.

"Cool," Jeremy said again.

"All right, let's strap in."

◆　◆　◆

The best days are those that unfold in ways never imagined nor even dreamed. And for the first time since his failed attempt to get to Fire Island, the memory of which was never far from his conscious thought, like the dull pain of a nagging injury, Jeremy followed Roy, his strife quickly forgotten.

"Which one?" Jeremy asked, pointing to the two seats.

"Unless you know how to fly this thing I suggest the front one."

Jeremy tentatively stepped onto the wing, held onto the hand grip, and climbed into the Stearman's front cockpit. It reminded him of climbing on the monkey bars on the playground as he sank deep into the guts of the airplane. It was as Roy said, a different animal, as if he'd inhabited the skin of some bizarre manmade creature, a product of man's desire for flight and man's observation of the animal world. It was an amalgam, part giraffe, part elephant, and as Jeremy looked out upon the yellow wings, even part bird.

Roy stepped onto the wing, reached into the cockpit, and securely fastened Jeremy into the seat. Jeremy heard and felt the cinch of the fabric straps drawing him into the belly of the beast. Sitting is one thing, strapped in quite another. Jeremy could feel the shoulder harness pressing against his shoulders, the lap belt pushing his hips squarely into the seat cushion, and for the first time in his life it occurred to him that his shoulders and hips were connected in some way.

"Comfortable?" Roy asked.

"Nope," Jeremy said with a smile.

"Good, you will be."

"I can't see anything in front of me!" Jeremy said. His head barely extended above the opening in the cockpit and the Stearman sat in a reclined position, the sky framed between the upper and lower wing.

"It gets worse." Roy placed a leather skullcap on Jeremy's head and secured the strap beneath his chin. The soft gel seals underneath the leather cap covered his ears. Roy gently placed the boom mike that extended from the cap's side against Jeremy's upper lip. The everyday sounds of life disappeared and a quiet stillness of the likes he'd never experienced even in dream washed over him. He could hear the silence within.

"Too snug?" Roy asked.

"What?!"

"Good, supposed to be."

"What's this?" Jeremy asked, pointing to the small boom mike. Roy ignored his question, approvingly tapped twice on the top of Jeremy's leather skull, and disappeared out of view.

The late afternoon sun shone through the small raked windscreen atop the fuselage. Jeremy was unable to see beyond the nose of the aircraft. A small portion of the propeller stuck up above the fuselage and looked about as useful as a hood ornament. *How can you fly if you can't see?* To his right and left the yellow wings of the Stearman framed the expanse of farmland like some idyllic postcard. The red tractor, the farmhouse, the mill house, the tall oak trees defining property's end, and the dent in the treeline's foliage where Jeremy had appeared from the depths of the San Souci Swamp in what seemed a lifetime ago.

Jeremy smiled and looked at the gauges a half-arm's length away. They were motionless, as still as he was still, each hand within its gauge pointed to its respective zero. But their purpose when built was not to be on zero, and neither was Jeremy's on this day.

Attached below the top wing, Jeremy saw a clear tube jutting downward with a red "E" inscribed at its base. It reminded him of the thermometer his mom would put under his tongue when fever hit. Above the "E," the fractions ¼, ½, and ¾. A small silver ball floated behind the etched "F." *No thirds, quarters.* He heard Kelli's voice: "One day you'll need to know how to divide," and he chuckled.

"Clear prop!" Roy yelled, and Jeremy heard "Clear pop!" *Father?* The thought left him as quickly as the engine groaned and spat smoke, as if annoyed to be awakened. Jeremy was familiar with the sound, the smell, the fury of this engine. The earth shook, the propeller stammered, then stuttered and reluctantly turned, obedient to the coughing demands from the blackish-gray smoke of the Lycoming engine. It poured into the open cockpit, clouding Jeremy's eyes and filling his lungs. He couldn't see beyond his nose, but he didn't close his eyes nor stop drawing fumes into his lungs. Exhaust just like the tractor's. He smiled. *This is no dream.*

Above the discordant clamor of the engine Jeremy heard Roy's voice in his headphones as clear as Principal Young calling Jeremy to his office at James Monroe Middle School. "It will clear in a second," Roy said. But he was not in school, and not in trouble. Here there were no walls, no doors, no principal; the only principles in play were those of physics.

As directed, the engine stirred mightily from cough to growl and the smoke dissipated. The shaking yielded to the rhythmic beat of internal combustion, the spinning propeller a ghost of itself. The gauges were no longer pegged at zero, and neither was Jeremy. He smiled wide. *This is not a dream. This is fucking cool!* Jeremy tentatively extended his hand outside the cockpit. The wind was forceful but not furious, and his hand was not ripped from his body as he thought it might have. He giggled.

"Do you see the mirror attached to the upper wing?" Roy asked. Jeremy looked and saw the small circular mirror attached to the upper wing, facing rearward. It reflected Roy's image, his bobbing head in a skull cap just above the opening in the rear cockpit.

"You all right?" Roy asked.

"Yes!" Jeremy yelled.

"No need to shout. Two ways to communicate: the first is a thumbs up or thumbs down in the mirror. The second is on the throttle next to your left arm. On it is a metal switch. Push up to talk. Got it?"

Jeremy clumsily found and then pushed up on the metal switch. "Got it," he said, his voice amplified; it was as if he were hearing it for the first time. This was the same voice he heard in his own head, the voice that cast doubt on his life, his future, his very existence. But this time it sounded different—joyous, firm, hopeful, and . . . true. He liked it.

Roy advanced the throttle and the Stearman lumbered forward with the haste of a lethargic elephant. It didn't know bike speed, skateboard speed, or even tractor speed, and Jeremy doubted that this machine could take flight when it could barely move at the tractor's pace.

What Jeremy didn't realize was that the ground beneath is uncertain, the sky above assured only if the earth permits. The Stearman moved forward, unhurried, one way, and then the other and back again. Jeremy, for a moment, could see forward with every S turn. He felt every bump and every rise and smiled, vaguely familiar with the land from driving the tractor. They taxied to the far end of the farm and Roy turned the Stearman 180 degrees. The expanse of land, every last foot his family had owned for 150 years, disappeared in front of the nose of the aircraft. Jeremy got a last look at the tall oaks at property's end and for the first time the farm seemed unsettlingly small. Roy pushed the throttle forward and the engine roared, the plane bucking as if it wanted to break free of its own skin, but otherwise held in place. Jeremy looked at the mirror and saw Roy methodically scanning the instruments. He marveled in the "why" of it all and Roy's mastery of this beast. Back to idle. Back to calm.

"Run-up is good. You ready?" Roy asked.

"Um . . ."

"I'll take that as a yes."

Roy once again pushed the throttle forward, the control yoke buried against his crotch. The Stearman shook, a purposeful, surly shake. The engine turned growl to roar, forceful to furious, the propeller cut the indignant wind, and the lumbering elephant became a sprinting cheetah. Jeremy was pushed back into his seat as he watched "his" bike leaning against the farmhouse quickly pass behind the right wing. *This is not bike speed! Holy shit!* The tail lifted, the control yoke centered, and Jeremy saw a way forward. The familiar bumps eased as the plane rose gently above the permitting earth. Giraffe. Elephant. Cheetah. Bird. Too many metaphors and all of them inadequate.

Flight.

The tall oaks at property's end passed gently underneath the wing as the Stearman climbed effortlessly amid the approving sky. The earth permitted and the heavens revealed and Jeremy saw the living . . . living. Those things hidden by fences, gates, and privilege were finally exposed. Jeremy saw houses with pools and children swimming, houses with playgrounds and children climbing, houses with patios and barbeques and kids eating. A man walked to his car, a woman jogged on the sidewalk, a shopkeeper dumped the trash, a man rode his bicycle, people spilled out of the supermarket pushing shopping carts full of groceries, two elderly gentlemen smoked cigars and laughed on a park bench. *Laughing about what?* Jeremy wondered. He felt guilty, a voyeur peeking in on the lives of the living. But don't we do that in the everyday with feet firmly planted? He may have been seeing as God sees, but he didn't know as God knows. *What are they thinking, where are they going?*

It was a bicycle ride's view from the air and his attention was drawn both to the view and the machine that afforded it. He looked at the gauge labeled KNOTS and observed that the needle was between fifty and one hundred, but he was too excited to figure out the value of the five lines between the two numbers. He didn't know whether he was five feet or five miles above the earth. He looked at the gauge ALTITUDE, its two needles pointing to zero and five, and he was as perplexed by the thorny mathematics as he was excited.

He looked at the wings, convinced that this yellow slab of fabric, sheet metal, and wood had changed form now that they were in the air and riding upon it. He knew the wings shouldn't flap like those of a bird, but he didn't discount the thought. *They don't move. It looks no different. How can this be? Must be magic? No, and this is not a dream.*

Jeremy extended his hand outside the cockpit, and this time it took effort. His fingers outstretched, hand as wing, it rose and fell with every movement of his wrist. He felt what he did not see and wondered what he did not know. *Just like in a car. It's not magic.*

The rhythmic combustion of the Lycoming engine resonated throughout Jeremy's body as the exhaust, its spent horses, sped past the lower wing. The RPM gauge pointed to the red line scribed above the number 20, the airspeed gauge at 80. He barely understood the math of what these gauges were saying, but his body and youthful enthusiasm told him that this beast could go faster, higher, farther.

He saw no roads, no speed limits, no red lights, and no police.

"Freedom!" he shouted. "Freedom!"

But there were forces at play: invisible and unknown to the novice but there nevertheless, always to be balanced, always to be considered, and always in conflict. These words known to the aviator, lived by the aviator, and if ignored by the aviator he knows he will go the way of Icarus. Expressed in science, precise and quantified: lift, weight, thrust, drag. Expressed in layman's terms: up, down, forward, back. All brought together in one deed. One act. Call it flight. Call it life. Call it one and the same.

We *all* fly in dream and life.

Jeremy eyed the wing mirror and saw Roy scanning the instruments. Inside the cockpit the yoke, pedals, and throttle all moved to Jeremy's wonderment. Roy saw what Jeremy did not, felt what Jeremy did not, understood what Jeremy did not. He curbed the zeal of the roaring engine by reducing the throttle and leveled the wings by centering the yoke. The expansive horizon came in full view and, where permitting, earth and welcoming sky met, slightly below the nose of the aircraft; Jeremy saw the horizon's slight curve and earth's end.

The world is round. He believed now that he had seen for himself. Until this day he'd never queried the world. He'd never asked why the moon was so gray, the grass so green, the sky so blue, or why it was easier to pedal his bicycle in a lower gear. As the Stearman yearned for the sky, Jeremy's thoughts were fueled by this machine shedding light on the world below, the genius of the men who created it, and the knowledge required to achieve it. Roy banked the Stearman and the farm was in full view. Majestic in its permanence, humble in its nature. Jeremy saw the reflected image of Roy looking at a place that was more than just his property. *Home.* Jeremy now understood what was home. Working his way back from the farm to the San Souci Swamp, his eyes followed the train tracks to the sidewalks and familiar side roads until he found the steps leading to his basement apartment. *Shelter.* And he understood.

Land gave way to the Great South Bay, the late afternoon sun reflecting its lingering orange hue. The *Stranger* moved across the reflective water heading toward Fire Island. The vast bay could swallow the paltry *Stranger* if it wished but the ferry slogged forward toward its port of call.

Jeremy had gazed upon this distant island . . . often, as we have gazed upon the stars. It was familiar and comforting, but from a different viewpoint or simply a different day, as unknown and unfamiliar as the far side of the moon. Jeremy had never much thought of the far side of Fire Island nor even imagined that it did give way to the sea. The barrier island protected the mainland from the ravages of the Atlantic, he would find out. It was just a five-minute bike ride from one side to the other. Behind Fire Island was ocean and sky that met to define the horizon. Blue sky over deep-blue sea, and Jeremy saw the Atlantic for the first time. To his amazement, it extended farther than his eyes could see and his imagination could travel. *My goodness!*

"Which way are we heading?" Roy asked. His voice drew Jeremy's thoughts from what was over the horizon to what direction was the horizon. *Which way are we going?* Jeremy, a stranger to this new world, hesitantly pointed forward and looked in the mirror.

"That way," he said.

"I know," Roy laughed. "And what direction is that?"

"That way," Jeremy repeated with greater emphasis of voice and finger.

"What are they teaching you in school? Information. It's there. Find it."

Jeremy looked at the panel and read one instrument at a time. He stopped at the compass. It was the only instrument, he observed, where the numbers and letters constantly oscillated in a sea of liquid, making it difficult to read. *What good is that?*

"'That way' has a name," Roy said. "It's all right to be wrong. Keep looking."

The letter S floated unsteadily by the fixed pointer. "South, we're going south!"

"Good. And do your eyes tell you the same?"

Eyes? "I don't understand."

"The gauges tell you what the world around you is already telling you, if you're open to it. What do your eyes see?"

Jeremy saw the setting sun and for a moment it brought him to the day he beat up Big Mac. He saw himself sitting in the corner of the cafeteria, looking out the window, and watching as a small plane crossing the setting sun disappeared over the horizon. He wondered who had filled his seat. This time the sun set not outside a window but below the right wing, the great expanse of the island extending beneath the left wing and the Atlantic Ocean in front of him. *The sun sets in the west, the island extends to the east, and the ocean is to the south.* He laughed. The compass stated, the world concurred, and the magnificence of life, of living, of experiencing opened up to him.

"I see!" Jeremy said.

"You do? Then explain," Roy said. And Jeremy did.

"Outstanding," Roy said. "Outstanding."

Roy cut the throttle, lowered the nose, and banked the airplane toward the shoreline. It rose to greet them, the white tops of the waves spraying the salty sea air onto the light brown sand just a few feet below the wing as the island passed quickly before Jeremy's eyes. People joyfully walked, ran, and biked along the beach. Sand dunes and boardwalks came into view and quickly disappeared as the Stearman raced eastbound. Jeremy was too late to return the friendly waves of beachgoers. It was all happening too fast.

He saw a thick ocean of green trees among numerous houses and was surprised to see both on this barrier island. *People live here. I thought they only visited. Who can live in paradise forever?* The island was both desolation and civilization. Wilderness and development. It was not what he'd imagined, but nothing ever was. Then he saw it, as he had seen it in dream, as his mother had often mentioned in those moments of solitude and depression and hope.

Alone among sand and sea, away from house and boardwalk, a weathered bench with legs firmly entrenched in the sand. A bench for the weary explorer. A bench for those to glory in the magnificence of nature. A bench simply to rest and sit, its purpose on that day long ago . . . a beginning.

It passed as quickly as it had come into view. Gone. A memory and a mystery once again. *Is it the one?* Jeremy asked himself.

Roy suddenly pulled back on the yoke, the Stearman standing on its ghostly propeller, the Lycoming engine going from furious to downright nasty. Jeremy was pressed against the seat, his chest feeling the weight of God's presence. The incandescent moon filled his view as they raced toward it. He looked at the wing mirror to see the crazy old goat smiling as he piloted toward the heavens. Roy laughed as he saw Jeremy's outsized eyes reflecting back at him.

Fly me to the moon, Roy sang.
Let me play among the stars.
Let me see what spring is like on Jupiter and Mars.
In other words, hold my hand.

"In other words, Sarah, kiss me, my sweet Sarah. Kiss me," Roy sings.

Jeremy reached out to grab the moon with the innocence of the small baby's hands he had dreamed of, sprinkled with seeds from the flowers atop the reed grass. The small fingers that wiggled and clasped before helplessly clenching into an innocent fist. See your hands reaching out tonight.

For all its fury, even this wild beast couldn't outrun the weight of its own existence. Nothing built by the hands of man could. Thrust met drag, lift met weight, up met down, and in that magical moment, all opposites meet, all are one, all are none. That place where God reveals and reluctantly, begrudgingly, lets go, if only for a moment, and they're free . . . motionless. *Fly or fall. Find your way tonight.*

They were statue. They were monument. The sky and earth below their pedestal. They stood as David stood, like Christ on the cross, like *La Liberté éclairant le monde.* Confident but weary, human yet divine. There between opposites, where thought and action, life and not-life bring forth revelation, a view, a taste, a feel, a touch, of God and his wellspring of genius, if one such dares. It is there where literature is born and becomes a Shakespearean sonnet, where physics becomes E=MC2, where baseball becomes a Jeter jump throw and music becomes the warmth of Chopin's nocturnes. To the defiant, to the crucified, to the rebels. *This isn't a dream.* The world revealed, if only for a second, Jeremy was speechless, in awe of the moment. Motionless. Transcendent.

The moon lessened, the earth called. The Stearman fell backward upon itself. We are all of this earth. We all fall.

Earthbound.

Roy kicked the tail, and the Stearman, with the refined movements of a ballet dancer, pirouetted on its left wing. The moon behind and Fire Island in full view, the seat straps pressing on Jeremy's body. Time and space had returned. Wonder transformed into a pure, contagious, meaty laughter from deep within Jeremy's belly.

The dunes in full view, they raced toward earth. "Time to go home," Roy said calmly. He throttled the Lycoming to idle, pointed the Stearman's nose toward the bay, and leveled the wings with such grace and ease Jeremy thought he was dreaming. *This is not a dream.*

The evening's fading twilight settled over the world and all was languid and peaceful. The earth, the sun, and the moon had a new meaning in Jeremy's life besides warmth, light, and the rise and fall of the tides. Bathed in whisky, the compass shook, the pilot steady, his passenger fueled by wonder and certainty. Nothing was as before. On this day the uncertain sprawl of adulthood had now been charted. He knows. He knows. He knows. The Stearman hurtled homebound accompanied by a thread of birds flying below the right wing. *Not above, but below!* Jeremy marveled. *Below!*

CHAPTER 21

fire island

THE *STRANGER* MADE ITS WAY from the Bayport Marina to the open waters of the Great South Bay. Jeremy and Kelli sat on the open bow deck as the ferry's air horn bellowed its departure to all who heard its blast. From afar, the *Stranger* appeared swift and graceful, yet up close Jeremy found it lumbering and noisy. The grumble of the ferry's engines gently resonated throughout his body and reminded him of both the tractor and plane. It also awakened a long-lost childhood memory of his mother pushing his stroller along the rough cement sidewalks to the unemployment office. The mind forgets but the body always remembers. Movement.

Once again, the ferry was filled with campers, bikers, fishermen, beachgoers, rowdy college students, gay lovers, and families of every color and stripe. They smiled and laughed as Jeremy looked at Kelli.

"How you doing?" Jeremy asked.

"Good, as long as this thing doesn't sway and roll."

"Do you want to know why we're going?"

"Are you ready to tell me?"

"I am," he said. He began, and by story's end he spoke of his recent good fortune befriending her and Roy.

She reached out and held his hand. "Jeremy, remember when I told you about how I like history?"

"I do."

"And you went blah, blah, blah."

"Yeah."

"The past will reveal itself today and so will the unexpected," she said.

"Witch talk?"

"Witch talk. For your exploits and bravery I bestow upon you the Thane of Glamis."

"What's that?"

"Look it up."

"Shakespeare?" he asked.

"Yep."

"Damn. I knew it. I will look it up. I promise. Today I just want to sit there and see what happens." He stood up from the deck chair and walked to the ferry's railing. The fresh, crisp air comforted his growing anxiety. He knocked inquisitively on the railing, ladder, and hull. In all the years he'd watched the ferry cross the bay it had never occurred to him to wonder what the boat was made of.

"It's made of cheese, just like the moon," Kelli said wryly.

"Steel. It's made of steel."

"And what did you think it was made of?"

"I would have bet on wood. Wood floats."

"So, you thinking of building one?"

"Why doesn't this thing sink to the bottom of the bay?" he said under his breath.

"I'm sure you'll find out."

As the *Stranger* reached open water, Jeremy leaned over the metal railing, the cross currents of the bay water reflecting the sun's rays, which made portions of the mysterious island look as if they were on fire.

He laughed at his new discovery, looked back toward the mainland, and found the crooked cedar pitch pine among the catbrier and Indian grass. A slight breeze swayed the vegetation and it opened to his castle in the sand. Jeremy smiled, said hello, and waved good-bye.

He looked up to see the captain. One hand was on the tiller, the other rested on the throttle, and a large compass guided both. The smokestack spewed a trail of diesel exhaust and the crew moved to the sound of his orders. It couldn't be piloted alone.

Fire Island, no longer a distant strip of land, rose from the sea and came into full view. It stood to meet him as if waiting centuries for his arrival. This was his port of call, his destination he'd looked at for endless summers from afar, from above and now in person. This island, which his mother had so often spoken of, as foreign to him as the Serengeti and as remote as the far side of the world, was now just a few steps away.

"Ready?" Kelli asked.

"Ready."

The thump of land and boat met as the ferry docked. Jeremy felt the smack of thought and reality coming together as if the drawbridge lowered to connect both worlds.

Kelli's hand touched his. A life preserver bringing Jeremy back to the present. She guided him, hand in hand, off the *Stranger*. The sea air carried the hypnotic voice of the ocean and he knew he was close. The brownish-yellow wooden boardwalk, worn and uneven, groaned under the weight of the disembarked. It was discolored by sun, sand, and sea, and nothing built by the hands of man sat flush upon this sandy strip of earth. Everything was built on stilts a few feet above it. The ground here was uncertain, the space above assured only if the sea permitted. Looking back, Jeremy's eyes searched for the far shoreline, but the rush of excited passengers shoved them forward. They walked briskly, the boardwalk branching out into a vascular network for the living, the yellow wooden roads all leading to the emerald-blue sea.

Because. Because. Because. The sea air mixed with the lofty aroma of barbeque and the ocean's roar with the laughter of families. They passed by cottages, a number and name above each of their front doors. A sign made of shells and sand by the home's owner. Cottage #12, House of the Rising Sun, the waft of food and laughter louder and more delicious than the rest. *A good sign*, he thought as they walked past.

The Indian grass rose higher than Jeremy was tall and the dunes were as big as houses. He was transfixed but he pushed forward, Kelli pressing to keep up. With every step on the yellow wooden road the ocean's lioness roar increased until the path gave way to sand and sea and the vast expanse of the Atlantic Ocean. As far as he could see the ocean touched the sky. *How deep is the ocean, how high is the sky?* He marveled in its purity, in its grandeur, in its power to move him beyond the weight of his own existence.

"I can see why my mom likes this place," he said.

"Then speak to her," Kelli countered.

He heard his mother's voice mix with the rhythmic waves lapping against the shoreline—it's most beautiful, most beautiful.

"I wonder why she never brought me here," he said.

"Then ask her."

At the ocean's edge he picked up a stone. He wanted to throw it in anger, but when his hands bathed in the cold waters of the Atlantic Ocean and pulled the heat from his fingertips, curiosity trumped rage. *The ocean is colder than the bay. How deep is the ocean, how high is the sky?* He was moved by the size of the planet, the treasures it held, and his place in it. In either direction the beach stretched as far as he could see, and at his feet the receding waves provided fresh evidence of the abundance of life, from marine plants to crustaceans, jellyfish to seashells.

"Do you know that clams and squids are mollusks?" he asked Kelli as he tossed the stone in favor of the abandoned seashell of a long-dead cockle. "So different but the same."

"I didn't. What's in a name?"

"Make me a promise."

"And what's that?" she asked.

"Please don't call me that name again."

"I promise."

A small bird with a black and white head, gray body, and short legs feet deep in the wet sand squawked loudly at Jeremy and Kelli. They had unknowingly intruded on the bird's midday meal.

"What's your name?" Jeremy asked as its bright red eyes added to the fury of another loud, harsh squawk.

"Okay, okay, we're leaving," Jeremy said.

"That's a night heron," an elderly lady interjected with camera in hand.

"And how do you know that?" Jeremy asked.

"I'm a bird watcher. It's a hobby I picked up from my parents a long time ago on this very beach. Very rare, and probably migrated here from South America."

"Something that small can travel that far?" he asked.

"Sure. Fueled by worms, insects, and a whole lot of desire."

"Why do you think it came here?"

"It most likely stopped for food and rest and to enjoy the benefits of such a beautiful day just like us, but only the bird knows."

"You sure he's not lost?" he asked.

"Birds don't get lost. They follow the sun."

"And when the sun goes down?"

"The stars at night," she said. "They always know their way. And you, why are you here?" She looked at Kelli, who expected her look to change to the scorn that she endured from so many who saw her pregnant self. But to her surprise the woman smiled.

"Here to find a nest?" Kelli said.

"It's the nature of things," the woman said kindly. "We all need one.

Well, enjoy the day and wear some sunscreen," she said as she followed the heron toward the water, clicking away with her camera.

They parted, all leaving footprints in the wet sand, their shadows following dutifully behind. Jeremy looked up, reminded of the black heron and remembering the path of the yellow Stearman.

There is nothing more certain than fate, nothing wiser than nature. It was his fate that had led him to this place and his unknowing nature that drove him. Perhaps that which guided the heron drove Jeremy as well. Hunger, thirst, beauty, desire, or simply just infinite weariness—he did not know. What he did know was his great fortune in meeting those who helped him get to this island.

He faithfully followed the sun, the shoreline, and the Stearman's path eastward. With Kelli in hand they found the weathered bench that he'd seen from the air. Sky, sea, and sand filled their view as they sat, weary young travelers.

How deep is the ocean, how high is the sky? Questions of wonder abounded in his thoughts. His life, this place, this world. They walked countless miles, taking in the joys of the island, and it was as he had dreamed—long summer days where families shared the sun, sand, barbeque, and each other's company. It brought him to his mother. *Just once, just once and maybe things would have been different.* He knew his mother's love was imperfect but that she loved him in the best way that she knew how.

Kelli sat, eloquent in her silence. It was his day. They sat for an hour as he digested his past. By hour's end anger had left, wonder and trust had firmly taken root. It wasn't Fire Island that changed Jeremy. It was his life up to this point, Fire Island the end of a chapter. He would write the next chapter, as he now realized he had written the previous one. To fight the good fight, to make his own way, to not end up in the Dead Sea.

"I'm good," he said.

"You sure? If you need more time—"

"I'm good. One thing."

"What's that?"

"Thanks," he said.

She laughed. "You're welcome."

"What's so funny?"

"I thought you were going to ask permission to kiss me, this place is so damn romantic."

"And if I had?"

"I would have knocked you on your ass," she said.

"You're that good a kisser?"

They started on their long trek back to the pier and the *Stranger*, Jeremy returning to a world as unfamiliar as the one they were leaving.

The weathered bench made of Long Island chestnut oak, a welcome respite for the enthused visitor, sat vacant by the sea, its legs firmly entrenched in the sand. Where earth met wood and where oak met sand, an inscription by two wayward lovers from long ago. The crudely engraved names faded as quickly as the passion, CLARE and MJ encircled in a heart.

Seagulls cawed, dived, and darted at one another, fighting for the last remnant of a freshly dead octopus washed upon the shore as the sun took its daily bow and the *Stranger* made its way home.

CHAPTER 22

salisbury steak

JEREMY SAT AT the kitchen table, his unfrozen dinner of Salisbury steak and corn untouched. The fruit of his mother's freshly cashed unemployment check. Compared to the typical meal of mac and cheese, minced beef made to resemble steak was a delicacy. But this was no common day. He was famished but his mind was buzzing from the day's events. Jeremy looked at Clare, who was absorbed by another senseless television program.

"It's all right, Mom. It's okay that you never took me to Fire Island."

"Fine, honey, fine," she replied, not turning eye nor ear toward her son.

"Mom, you're not listening."

"I am honey, really."

Jeremy put down his plastic forkful of processed meat and rehydrated corn and walked in front of the television. "I went to Fire Island today," he said.

"You did? School event?"

"It's Saturday, Mom."

"Oh. Did you enjoy yourself?"

"I did."

"Great, now go eat your dinner before it gets cold."

"Mom, this isn't an interview with your unemployment counselor."

"If there's something going on then you need to tell me!" Clare said, her full attention now focused on her son.

"I have a friend in school. A girl."

"A girl? Do you . . . *like* her?"

"I do," Jeremy said.

"That's great. And you went with her to Fire Island?"

"Yes," Jeremy said.

"I'm glad you're making friends. She *is* a friend, right?"

"Yes."

"What's her name?"

"Kelli. She's pregnant."

"What? No! Please no! Not you! Not my son! Damn it! How could you! I wanted better for you! How could you do this to me! To make the same mistake—"

Clare caught herself but a few words too late. It hung like the heavy scent of the microwaved meat.

"Mistake? Anyway, it wasn't me," Jeremy said.

Clare turned off the television. "I didn't mean that, sweetie."

"Fire Island is as beautiful as you said."

"I was a frightened teenager. I thought this happened to other girls. Not me!"

"It's okay, Mom."

"What does a sixteen-year-old girl know about love?"

"I'm proud of you, Mom. You've done the best you can. I want you to know that. But you owe yourself a chance—to be bigger than this, better than this. You owe me nothing, and I won't be an excuse for you sitting on that couch."

"*Owe* you? I'm *responsible* for you! Excuses? You have no idea!"

"You owe yourself a chance," Jeremy repeated.

"And your 'chance' is with a pregnant girl? Really?"

"I told you, she's a friend."

"Then why don't you explain it to me, in your sixteen years of infinite wisdom on this earth," Clare said, her voice rising.

"I'm fourteen, Mom."

Clare rolled her eyes. "Even better."

"You gave up on yourself. Time to step up."

"You're my son, my blood, my life. I have stepped up!" she yelled.

Jeremy heard her last words trail off without the strength of truth into a handful of tears. He stepped forward, kissed her on the forehead, told her that he loved her, and walked to his room hungry no longer.

PART II

CHAPTER 1

one of us club

"*BACON!*" JEREMY EXCLAIMED, his attention divided between bush-hogging the grass and the gathered crowd preparing an early morning breakfast in front of the barn. His nostrils flared as he took in the fragrant mix of bacon and diesel exhaust and tapped the tractor's frame, its large wheels creating a wake of cut grass as they headed toward the barn. "Who are those people, Harvester?" he asked out loud.

"Two slices of bacon, Gus," Roy said.

"One," Gus replied. "Your cholesterol."

"Two! I've had two pieces of bacon for eighty plus years! Why change now?"

"Give him two!" Lewis said. "We outlived our wives. If they didn't kill us, bacon sure the hell won't!"

"Give him a whole side of bacon if it'll shut him up," Cliff said.

"Death must have been a party for those poor women, after living with you clowns," Betty cracked.

The Wednesday regulars sat at a long wooden table outside the hay barn as Gus and Betty served farm-fresh grilled eggs, thick slices of applewood-smoked bacon, and hash browns. The warmth of the early morning sun and fresh air made for another memorable

Breakfast Wednesday, a Higgins family tradition going back 150 years. At first it had served the practical purpose of communicating between farms well before the telephone and just after the invention of the wired telegram. Discussions varied from crop rotation to the weather, the terrible cost of the Civil War, or simply catching up with neighbors. But its most important function was to help fellow farmers and neighbors in need. Farmer helping farmer and family helping family, all trying to get through a harsh winter or a bad harvest. But as time passed and the comforts created by technology made life easier, Breakfast Wednesdays gatherings turned to gossip and little more.

With Sarah in the nursing home, Betty was the last of the women in the group. Like clockwork, she arrived in her Venetian red '57 Corvette at daybreak. She'd only had two cars in her lifetime and both were '57 Vettes. After accidently jumping a few curbs when she was seventy, she knew that something had to change. Her aging arthritic legs sometimes failed pressing on the taut three-speed clutch trying to corral the 245-horsepower engine. Slowing down or giving up were not in her vocabulary, so she simply made an even trade for another '57 Vette with a Powerglide automatic transmission. Problem solved—well, almost. It was cascade green and, as she told her three adult children at their next dinner gathering, "Momma don't drive green so this beautiful meal I've cooked for you is going to cost you ten grand divided by three." They grudgingly paid for the expensive paint job and ten years later still laughed at the will of a woman who always lived her life in the fast lane with the big boys. Now eighty, she had outlived four husbands, and being around a group of adolescent male seniors was pure entertainment for her.

The current group went back as far as its oldest member, Lewis, who was pushing ninety. His grandson had dropped him off before heading to work and Betty would drive him back to his son's house at day's end.

"I can't believe you let her drive you home," said Cliff, a spry seventy-year-old who constantly spilled insults and whose brain (or what was left of it), the others were convinced, had been swallowed by his tongue. "She's eighty and that's a whole lot of car. You losing your mind, you crazy old bastard, or did they take that out with your prostate?"

"I got more organs left than you!" Lewis said.

"He's right," Dixon said, laughing. Dixon's bellicose laugh was all he could muster from the constraints of his wheelchair. Not all had aged as well as Lewis, but they all came to Breakfast Wednesdays by any means possible. Some came from the retirement homes, some from their own homes, and some from their children's homes.

Dixon was a product of the segregated South who had no taste for the indignities of separate water fountains or the limits on one's opportunity. He discovered Long Island in his twenties, made a good life for himself, and never left.

"You shouldn't be laughing," Cliff said. "At least I don't pee on myself, Diaper Man."

"It's Depends Man!" Dixon said. "Enemy of the leaky bladder! Superhero for truth, justice, and the American diaper!"

"All right there, you crazies, who's saying grace today?" Roy asked.

"Me," Cliff quickly replied.

"No, you always say grace," Roy said.

"But I have visions."

"That's your medication, Prophet," Betty said.

"How 'bout Alter Boy?" Roy asked. A collective groan went up from the group, Gus reminded of the complaint he'd heard for the last fifty years.

"Okay, okay. I'll keep it short," Gus said.

"Remember, brevity is a sign of genius," Cliff said.

"Remember, brevity is a sign of Jesus," Betty reminded Gus.

"Food's getting cold!" Dixon said.

"Remember, God is not on your timetable," Gus said.

"*Gus!*" Roy said.

This was the "One of Us" club, or what was left of it. They were once kids who were born poor and served their country in peace and war, and as they prospered so did the nation. The motley One of Us club had seized upon the opportunities afforded by both their individual efforts and their generation's collective energy. They took risks and launched programs like the GI Bill, Social Security, and Medicare, knowing that they would secure a better life and a more prosperous country for themselves and all who followed. A better life than they had ever dreamed of when they were children. But this was not a dream.

Most were from Long Island, but others had come to settle here from all parts of the country. They all married, some divorced, some with children, others childless, and all experienced both tragedy and triumph. Now in the twilight of life, they planned on finishing out their lives in the place they loved among people they loved. This group wasn't made of the wheelchair-bound has-beens medicated to a stupor and waiting to die in assisted living facilities. This group defied death.

The only requirements of the One of Us club were a long life and tall tales, and not necessarily in that order. Breakfast greased conversations going back as far as they could remember or fabricate. Their solemn vow was simple: "the last of the herd still standing" would change the title atop the hay barn to the "None of Us Left Club."

The table set and plates full, Gus stood and heads bowed. For those no longer living—and there were many—a place setting was always set at the end of the table.

"In nomine Patriset Filii et Spiritus Sancti," Gus said.

"English, Gus! English!" Cliff yelled.

"Latin is the language of the Catholic Church!" Gus said.

"I'm not Latin!" Cliff yelled. "I'm hungry!"

ONE OF US CLUB

"Okay, okay. In the Gospel According to Saint John, Jesus shall give his disciples a well of water springing up into everlasting life."

"Everlasting life, my ass!" Dixon yelled.

"I wear Depends and pee on myself," Cliff said. "Don't talk about water. Come on!"

"That's it! I'm saying grace," Lewis said. "Lord, bless this bunch before they munch."

"Amen!" the group said.

"I hope you're all proud of yourselves," Gus said. "That's an improvement from 'Rub a dub dub, thanks for the grub.'"

"Amen!" the group repeated.

"Congratulations, Gus, that was your best grace yet," Cliff said.

As heads rose to begin eating the tractor came in full view.

"My God, a vision!" Cliff said.

"Relax, Buddha. We all see him," Betty said.

Jeremy drove the tractor to the side of the barn, shut it down, jumped off, and walked toward Roy.

"Good morning," Jeremy said, and the group replied with their hellos.

"How's it running?" Roy asked.

"Great," Jeremy said.

"Then why'd you stop?"

"I've got to get going to school."

"He wants breakfast, Roy," Betty said. "Can't you see the kid's hungry?"

"Hungry? I've been wanting to drive that tractor for forty years," Cliff said. "Son, who are you?"

"My Lord, I've been replaced. I thought I would cut—" Gus said.

"Relax, both of you," Roy said. "This is Jeremy. Since I've been spending more time at the nursing home, I needed some help around here. You got a problem with that?"

133

"Jeremy, how'd you two meet?" Betty asked.

Jeremy looked at Roy.

"Feed him, Betty, that's not important," Roy said.

"Oh, yes it is," Cliff said. "You haven't made a new friend in fifty years, you old curmudgeon."

"Come on kid, tell us," Dixon said, and Jeremy looked at Roy again.

"Well, go ahead, tell them," Roy said. "But give them the short version—your food's getting cold."

Betty sat Jeremy down at the end of the table, facing the empty place setting for those no longer living.

"Um, well, um—" Jeremy said.

"No secrets here, kid," Betty said. "From the beginning."

"He ran me over with the tractor, thought he killed me, but I survived and he offered me a job." The group howled in laughter as a famished Jeremy devoured his meal.

"If that's the only way you'll let me drive your tractor, I guess I don't want to anymore," Cliff said.

"My God, son, when was the last time you ate?" Betty asked.

"Breakfast?" Jeremy asked.

"Any meal."

"Last night, macaroni and cheese."

"Lord, Gus, give him seconds," Betty said.

"Shouldn't you be in school, young man?" Cliff asked.

"Yes, sir, I'm going now," Jeremy answered.

"And what school do you go to?" Betty asked.

"Frontier," he said.

"Isn't that the school where convicts go?" Lewis asked.

Jeremy didn't respond.

"Answer the man," Roy said.

"I got into a fight and they sent me there," Jeremy said.

"Bully?" Cliff asked.

"Yes, sir."

"Who won?" Cliff asked.

"No, no, the Lord—" Gus said.

"Screw that turn-the-cheek bullshit," Cliff said. "Did you win?"

"Time to go to school," Roy said. "You can finish up this afternoon."

"Yes, sir," Jeremy said.

"Don't mind them, Jeremy. They're just harmless old men just having fun," Betty said as she walked him to his bicycle by the barn.

"Yes, ma'am. None taken," Jeremy said.

"Roy doesn't let anyone drive his tractor," Betty said.

"And he took me for a ride in his plane and gave me this bicycle."

"Really? Well, he must think highly of you."

"Do you think so?"

"I do," she said.

Jeremy got on his bike and started pedaling toward school.

"My God, that convict's stealing your bicycle!" Lewis said.

"Wrong again, genius," Betty said. "Wrong again."

CHAPTER 2

poetry

"FOCUS!" KELLI SAID. "FOCUS!"

"Okay, okay," Jeremy said. "I need—"

"You haven't even—"

"Help me change my password."

"You know—"

"Please," Jeremy said.

"Ugh. Now I'm the distraction. Okay. But you promise—"

"I'll do my work."

Kelli moved from her desk to his to the chagrin of Collins and the security guard. She threw them her pregnant annoyed look and they quickly retreated, one behind the *Times*, the other behind his *Truck Round-Up* magazine.

Mouse and keyboard: Home screen. Settings $\longrightarrow$ Control Center $\longrightarrow$ Password $\longrightarrow$ Change.

"What's the new password?" Kelli asked.

"Harvester," he said. She typed it in. UNABLE, the computer responded. She pointed to the screen. Minimum eight characters, numbers and letters, no space.

"Harvester1935," he said. She typed it in. Accepted. Collins's computer beeped. The paper curtain came down and he looked at the two with suspicion but returned to reading the obits.

"What's that?" Kelli asked.

"The tractor I told you about on the ferry. Promise you'll let me show you?"

"1935?"

"Yeah."

"Can't be," she said.

"Can be. Your witch powers seem to be fading. Today, after school."

"Stand up and I'll kick you in the balls," she said with a smirk. "You'll see my powers at work."

"It's only a few miles from here," he said. "No ferry."

"Promise me you'll focus and get your work done?"

"I promise," he said.

He opened up the science module and mollusks and crustaceans now meant more than just a name. He tried and she saw him trying. When he got stuck she felt his look, a look of genuine trust that she would help. And help she did. She freed him of feeling stupid. It was, she said, about welcoming the unknowns of learning and not being embarrassed by the complexities that reveal the world through science, math, history, and other subjects.

From that day on the two were inseparable. It cost Jeremy the vanilla side of his ice cream sandwich and Kelli the unconstrained chatter among the girls at the Bridge Way House. Both found their sacrifices to be more than worth it. They shared in each other's world. For Jeremy, school was no longer a place of poor grades and trouble.

He struggled but was determined, a determination to learn now that the world and how it works interested him. A door opened by his own hand and with the help of others because all is connected. He read and completed module after module, from math to geography, English to science. And when his eyes went vacant and his mind wandered, Kelli leaned over and ignited a spark of determination and focus. He learned that mathematics could describe music, how geology was the reason for geography and the written word, how plain English could be expressed not only in a dearth of anger but also rise above the muck into the magical wispy airs.

School over, Kelli waited at the bicycle rack, iPad mini in hand.

"What's with the iPad?" Jeremy asked.

"You're having trouble with language."

"Not language, poetry. I don't know why we have—"

"Poetry is just English in verse and rhyme," she said. "You'll read, I'll drive. My ass is still hurting from our last jaunt to the pier. Just show me the way."

The luggage carrier on the Schwinn made for an uncomfortable but convenient seat. Jeremy put his sweater on the flat metal rack and sat. Kelli screwed her face into a scowl.

"What?" he asked.

"Men," she said. "You could have offered me that sweater when we went to the pier."

"You sure you—"

"Which way!" she said as she mounted the bicycle.

"And what about Carol?"

"Miss Carol has a favorite saying: she's my guardian, not my guard. Let's go!" Kelli said and started pedaling away from the school. Jeremy wrapped one of his arms around Kelli's waist and held the iPad mini in the other. Comfortably close, he felt the radiant warmth of her body and the growing life inside her. She adjusted his hand above her belly and just below her growing breasts.

"Sorry," he said.

"No need to apologize, though you're probably enjoying this."

"I . . . am," he said. He felt joy in her friendship and pleasure in her touch. As he pressed tighter, body touching body, his body warmed and he laughed a nervous laugh.

"What's so funny?" Kelli asked.

"Thanks for sharing the afternoon with me."

"That's not funny! You dork! Yes, those are my breasts and belly you're touching—if you didn't hold on you'd fall off, dickweed! This isn't your master plan of getting a cheap feel, is it?"

"No, ma'am," he said, the "ma'am" an unconscious response to the scolding. "You're the one who wanted to be up front." His face was red as he experienced the stinging rebuke of a young lady for the first time in his young life. *Good God, she could read my mind. She* is *a witch.* Jeremy was thankful to be on the back of the bike where he could hide the color of his skin brought on by the beat of his heating heart.

"Read!" she said. "Read!"

Poetry had meant little to Jeremy, but he knew there was something there, something he'd dismissed before he'd met Kelli. But now he wanted it to open up to him, even if only grudgingly so.

"Okay, okay. 'A noiseless, patient spider,'" he recited. "'I mark'd, where, on a little promontory, it stood isolated.' What's a promontory?" he asked.

"A rock outcropping sticking out into the ocean," she said.

"'Mark'd how, to explore the vacant, vast surrounding, / It launch'd forth filament, filament, filament, out of itself; / Ever unreeling them—ever tirelessly speeding them.'"

"Stop," she said. "What does that verse mean?"

Jeremy read it again, silently this time. "Filament? A spider spins it web. What—"

"Excellent. Continue."

"This is like a puzzle. I like it. 'And You, O my Soul, where you stand / Surrounded, surrounded, in measureless oceans of space. / Ceaselessly musing, venturing, throwing, seeking the spheres, to connect them.' Musing?" he asked.

"Thought, reflection."

"'Till the bridge you will need, be form'd-till the ductile anchor hold.' Ductile?"

"Stretchable."

"'Till the gossamer thread you fling, catch somewhere, O my Soul.' Gossamer?"

"Spider's web," she said. "What does it mean to you?"

Jeremy's first thought was of her. *I'm in this girl's web. I love her. Don't say that, idiot.*

"It compares a spider to a . . . human."

"Good. In what way?"

"A spider spins its web. A person creates their own life."

"Good. And for what reason?"

"For the spider to catch food—and depending on the person, to lie, cheat, steal, or bully."

"Not in this poem."

"Says who?" Jeremy exclaimed. "You said that a poem means what I decided that it means!"

"'And You O my soul where you stand,'" Kelli recited. "Haven't we connected? Haven't you reached out and created your own web, of friends, of knowledge, of perseverance, and the courage to go forward?"

"I'm trying."

"I know. Fire Island."

"Fire Island."

"Just like the spider."

"Just like the spider."

He held tighter to her bosom and belly as if the truth lay inside her. She steered the bicycle, asking for direction when needed, and told Jeremy to read the second poem aloud as she recited from memory, their voice one:

"'No man is an island, / Entire of itself / Every man is a piece of the continent, / A part of the main. / If a clod be washed away by the sea, / Europe is less. / As well as if a promontory were.'"

"Left at the corner?" she asked.

"Yes, at the corner."

"'As well as if a manor of thy friends / Or of thine won were: / Any man's death diminishes me, / Because I am involved in mankind, / And therefore never send to know for whom the bell tolls; / It tolls for thee.'"

"Through the intersection?" she asked.

"Yes," said Jeremy.

"Poetry, Jeremy," she said. He rested his head against her back, his eyes squeezed closed and focused on his breathing. He felt every word created in her chest, pressed upward from her diaphragm and given birth by her self-assured voice.

"Poetry," she repeated.

"Who would have thought," he said, his voice cracking with emotion and puberty. "Thanks."

"You're welcome. Which way?"

"Next ri—right."

The gravel road began where the yellow-striped paved road ended. Kelli bicycled down the winding road as Jeremy gathered himself in silence. As they passed the tall oaks surrounding the edges of the farm, Kelli looked around at the expanse of land, the old barns, the vintage aircraft, and Roy's picturesque home.

"My God Jeremy, it's beautiful. How did you find this place?"

"By accident," he said softly.

"Who's the owner?"

"Roy Higgins."

"And he gave you the bike?"

"Not exactly. Over there next to the tractor."

Kelli pulled up next to the barn.

"We bartered," Jeremy said. "I cut the lawn to pay for the bicycle. This is my job . . . for now."

Kelli whistled. "That's a lot of grass. It must take you weeks!"

"Nah," he said, pointing to the tractor. "Not with this guy."

"Are you kidding me?"

"Nope. Ready for another ride?"

"Wow. Are you sure you can—"

"Yep, Roy taught me," he said proudly. He jumped on the tractor, pulled out the choke, pressed the clutch, tapped the gas, and turned the key. The tractor rumbled to life. Kelli, startled, took a step back.

"No worries," Jeremy said over the growl of the engine. He offered his hand and she tentatively stepped up on the tractor and sat next to him.

"Awesome!" she said.

"Ready to cut some grass?"

"Ready!"

Jeremy put the tractor in gear and it rumbled forward, grass flying in their wake. Kelli drew in a deep breath, and in the joy of the moment stood up and yelled.

"This is awesome, Jeremy!" she screamed, her unbridled joy bringing a smile to his face. "Thank you for bringing me here!"

"Thank *you*," he said. They laughed together as he took her hand and put it on the steering wheel and covered it with his own.

"Where to?" she asked.

"The horizon," he said as he pointed to the uncut grass on the far end of the farm.

From the distant farmhouse where the windows were always open this time of year, the fresh spring breeze carried the rumble of the tractor and the distant yell into the kitchen. Roy, who was making tea for Sarah, looked up with concern. His aged eyes gazed through the window, a window framed in oak that was shaped with his grandfather's hands from trees felled on this farm. It was as if he was gazing up at the stars, at the vast universe stretched before his eyes, and looking back in time. The kettle whistled. He didn't hear it. He simply stared at what he thought was his mind recreating a day lived long ago but never forgotten, the day he took Sarah for a ride on the tractor fifty years ago.

"Oh my," Roy said. He took off his glasses, as if they were betraying him. After a thorough inspection he saw that they weren't damaged nor dirty and put them back on, the vision still framed in the window, Roy's memory unearthed by his irrational eyes. It took him a few seconds before he realized it was Jeremy and a young girl. He ignored reason and fell willingly into the narcotic comfort of the past.

"The ket . . . tle, Roy, the kettle," Sarah said, her voice bringing him back to the present.

"Of course, dear," he said and turned off the burner. The familiar sound of the kettle and frequent visits to the farm steadied Sarah's decline. Roy guided her to the window.

"Sweetie, do you see what I see?" he asked. Sarah looked out expressionless, and then somewhere in her collective memory, she remembered. Her eyes focused, her smile sweetened, and when she spoke, her voice sounded . . . young.

"Roy Higgins, is this the best you can do?"

"What do you mean?"

"I asked for a ride."

Roy pointed out the window at the tractor. "That is a ride."

"In a car, not a tractor! A ride to town for dinner and a movie. I didn't come over to help you with your chores," she said with vigor, astonishing Roy, who was almost convinced that his ears were failing him as well. He heard no hesitation or stuttering and her voice was as young as the day he'd met her. He took her hand and they walked out onto the porch.

Jeremy stopped the tractor in the middle of the field and shut off the engine. They sat in silence watching the blue jays chirping, the trees slightly swaying in a wisp of wind, and the hungry squirrels chewing on pinecones.

"What are you thinking?" Jeremy asked.

Kelli felt the life inside her as she felt the discomfort of life and death as part of the everyday cycle of the farm. She knew that few farm animals don't die of old age; their destiny at birth is the slaughterhouse, and for those who fall sick, compost for the garden. But in her youthful wisdom she felt the sanctity of life at this farm more so than any other place she'd ever been. She exhaled with both relief and anxiety.

"I'm not as strong as you think. I'm scared, Jeremy. What will become of my child? This thing growing inside of me."

"You're calling it a thing? Don't you know if it is a—"

"I told the doctor that I didn't want to know."

"Why not?"

"I know it's a boy. I feel it's a boy. It becomes more familiar by the day. And every day I worry more than the last."

"You'll be a great mom, I know you will."

"But his father, Jeremy. He has no father."

"He'll wonder, he'll be angry, but I know—"

"He'll be angry at me," she said.

"Yep, at times, but with you as his mom he won't carry it as long as I did. I don't worry anymore. He doesn't matter. At least to me he doesn't. I left all that for the seagulls to fight over on Fire Island."

"That's big stuff, Jeremy."

"Waiting for him was like waiting for my life to begin. No more waiting, no more wondering. What will happen to me now has nothing to do with him. Your son will be fine."

"How do you know that?"

"Because he'll have you," he said.

"But—"

"Please, let me finish. When I first saw you I thought things—ugly things—about you, but then you forced me to know you."

"Forced?" she asked.

"Okay, that's not the right word. You *challenged* me to get to know you. And as you said I would, I got to know myself. You'll be fine, Kelli. You helped me and I can help you. I'll be here for you as you have for me. I promise. And we'll find our way together, whatever that might be," he said.

Kelli put her hands on top of his as he gripped the steering wheel, his knuckles whitened by the sincerity of his short speech. She reached over and kissed him on the cheek. He stared at her, unmoved.

"What?" she asked.

"My mother kisses me on the cheek. You're not my mother."

"Fair enough," she said. Kelli kissed her forefinger and pressed it against his lips. "Not good enough?" She took his hand and placed his forefinger against her lips and kissed it. The crickets chirped. He was silent and innocent. She was silent and experienced. She drew his finger into her mouth. His eyes grew large, his skin flushed, and his body froze. Kelli winked, slowly pulled his finger out of her mouth, and kissed him on the lips.

"Oh my!" Roy said.

"I re . . . m . . . ember. I remem . . . ber," Sarah said as they watched Kelli and Jeremy from the farmhouse porch.

"I don't remember it like that!" Roy said.

"Is that your friend?" Kelli asked.

"It is," Jeremy said. He started the tractor and drove up to the house. Sarah watched intently as Kelli walked onto the porch. There, in one's eyes, was a person's history, ageless and telling. Sarah stood still, looking and knowing. Kelli expressed her intuition with a smile and Sarah's grace moved her to gently take Sarah's hand and place it on her belly.

Sarah remembered. Too often we embellish our life story not for others but for our own sake. We alter it to fit our own narrative if only to endure our own shortcomings, our own tragedies. But as is often the case, it is the everyday that reminds us of the past, and the past isn't as sweet as we remember or can be changed as easily as we like. Sarah turned and looked at a nervous Roy as if to say, "I remember, Roy. I remember."

She remembered what it felt like to have another human growing inside of her, how it felt when she found out she was pregnant, what it felt like to have life kicking you from the outside and life kicking back from the inside and what it felt like to give birth to a child who will love you and whom you love more than anything in this world. Even if only for a few months. And it was all right to remember.

"A bo . . . y," she said, touching Kelli's belly. "A boy. You kn . . . ow."

"I do," Kelli said.

Sarah gently took Kelli's hand and led her to the vacant garden next to the house. Roy knew not to follow. It was her space, her place to remember. There, with some effort and help from Kelli, she found the small copper nameplate pressed flush into cement and level with the earth. And with stilted speech but a clear memory Sarah spoke about her pregnancy, her child's birth, and her child's death. Scarlet fever. Three months. When she was done they returned to the porch, Roy and Jeremy watching all the while.

"Sarah and I would like to replant the garden. We will start tomorrow," Kelli said matter-of-factly. "We'll start after school and we won't need your help."

"Yes, ma'am," Roy said with great deference to the pregnant red-headed sixteen-year-old he'd just met. "Yes, ma'am."

CHAPTER 3

the garden anew

AT DAYBREAK ROY KNEW what needed to be done. Before leaving for the nursing home he rummaged in the barn for Sarah's wheelbarrow and her gardening tools. He knew what the garden meant to Sarah and what working on it would do for her spirit and health. What he'd forgotten was what it would do for him. The garden hadn't been tilled in years. As Sarah's disease progressed, her interest in her much-loved garden waned. Its surface was strewn with weeds as coarse as barbed wire, the earth beneath was as dense as rock. It would be impossible for Sarah and Kelli to garden with a pickax and shovel. It had to be tilled.

The harvester unearthed the garden's rich bounty, returning it to its sweet, fresh, earthy smell and the cycle of life that Roy had long forgotten. The rich brown clumps of soil neatly aligned in cleanly cut furrows moved Roy to tears.

He was not done. He found his rusting tin can of Brasso metal polish and a discarded shirt in the depths of the barn. The abrasive-smelling ammonia and elbow grease slowly turned the tarnished brass plate back to its original coppery luster. It was okay to remember. Roy pressed his fingers against each raised letter of his son's name and with it a memory of those three months long ago. It was Sarah's wish to have his ashes interred on the farm. Roy, broken by the death of their newborn but knowing that her pain was far deeper than his, had thought it a bad idea but didn't protest. Now he smiled at her wisdom as he ran his hand over the nameplate.

"Roy Jeremiah Higgins IV, after great-great-grandpa," he said. He hadn't much thought of his grandfather's middle name and smiled at the coincidence. Thoughts of his own death crept into his mind, but he was having none of it. *Today is about life, not death, not about just surviving but living.*

Roy and Sarah waited on the porch and, as promised, Jeremy and Kelli arrived after school. Lined atop the neatly furrowed, tilled earth were Sarah's favorite plants and flowers. Seedlings of peas, corn, radish, greens, and onions along with herbs of yellow yarrow, cilantro, sage, and thyme. The vivid red and blue geraniums brought colorful flora to the garden.

"I know you said you didn't need help, but—" Roy said.

"It's beautiful, Mr. Higgins, just beautiful," Kelli said.

"Please call me Roy. If I had more time I'd have made a new scarecrow. That one doesn't look mean enough to scare any crows around here."

"Looks mean enough to me," Jeremy said.

"Kid, you don't know mean," Roy said. "That thing was made in China. What do they know about scarecrows?" On the last furrow overlooking the garden the scarecrow hung, nailed to its cross.

"All the garden needs now is planting, watering, and a little tenderness," Roy said.

"That it does," Kelli said.

"Nothing like Long Island corn; ain't a garden without it."

Kelli walked over to Sarah and led her to the garden. Roy watched with curiosity, hope, and expectation. As she had done for fifty years at garden's edge, Sarah slowly took off her shoes and socks and placed them where tilled soil met firm ground. She walked knowingly to garden's center and felt the rich warm soil between her toes and slowly bent her knees to the ground. With cupped hands she drew earth and lifted it upward. She spoke softly, haltingly, trying to remember, refusing to forget:

"May the soil . . . b— be ble— blessed . . . as the . . . wo womb . . . of the . . . land. Sa— say . . . sacred . . . the seeds. . . . Br— bring forth . . . the garden . . . a— a anew. . . .   Bless my son. . . . Ble bless . . . K— . . . Ke— Kel— . . . Kelli's . . . son. . . . Kelli's son.

"Amen," she said at prayer's end.

Jeremy watched as Roy mirrored her prayer under his breath. Roy knew her every word, his hopes fulfilled. She was still here in mind and spirit, even able to bless Kelli's son. Sarah slowly turned to Kelli and gestured for her to join her in the garden. With the enthusiasm of a child jumping into a pool, Kelli took off her shoes and socks, walked into the soil, and kneeled at Sarah's side. Sarah gave Kelli the first seedling and watched as she placed its roots into the drawn earth from which she had drawn her prayer. Knee-deep in soil, they started planting the seedlings and flowers.

"Well, should we go help them?" Jeremy asked.

"Son, you've planted enough seed," Roy said.

"But—"

"But nothing. How 'bout straight and level?"

"What's that?"

"Flying, let's go flying," Roy said.

"Really?!"

"You didn't destroy my tractor or throw up in the Stearman. That showed me something."

"Thanks," Jeremy said.

"Don't get full of yourself. When I let you solo on the harvester,

I taught, you listened, and you showed me you could properly work my tractor. Good head, good hands. Flying is a thinking man's game. Some have it up here"—Roy pointed to his head—"but some can't translate it to here," he said, spreading his fingers and turning his aged palms upward. "The question is, can you do the same in the Stearman. Well, can you?"

"I don't know."

"Do you want to find out?"

"Y—yes," said Jeremy.

"Why the hesitation? You scared?"

"No, I never dreamed I'd—"

"Kid, this ain't a dream," was Roy's terse response. "Learning to fly is hard work, and not that highfalutin Jonathan Livingston Seagull bullshit or that 'slipped the surly bonds of earth' nonsense."

"Yes, sir."

"Besides, I wouldn't offer if I didn't think you could do it."

"And if Kelli doesn't show up, will you still teach me?"

Roy paused before he said, "I would."

"Why the hesitation?"

"Sarah comes first, but I'm sure we can figure out a schedule."

"Promise?" Jeremy asked.

"What's a man's worth if his word means nothing? Promise. Daylight's burning."

Their promise sealed with a handshake, Roy and Jeremy pulled the Stearman out of the barn. Repetition bred familiarity as Roy built on the instruction from their first flight. The tanks were full, the gas cap tightened. Switches off and cockpit secure, the engine oil ample and a hue of gold. Seven turns of the prop and a syringe of fuel into the Lycoming's heart. The ailerons moving freely, the tires properly round, and the tail in good order. Every action was purposeful, every action had meaning, and every observation gave a verdict of airworthiness. Worthiness, a word Jeremy knew well. "Abstraction is for philosophers or poets, not pilots," Roy barked. "You're a quick learner. I bet you're good at school."

"When I'm interested," Jeremy said.

"Same here."

Strapped in, Roy gave a hearty "Prop clear!" and engaged the starter, and the Stearman came alive. Jeremy knew what to expect, his last flight informing the present. Wonder and joy were part of the experience, but now also expectation and responsibility. He had a thirst to learn but also not to disappoint. This man he once thought strange and crazy, this man who once threatened him with a crescent wrench, this man who knocked him unconscious with the blunt end of a tractor now afforded him an opportunity he'd never imagined nor even dreamed of. He was vested, all in, and smiled knowing so.

As they taxied away from the barn, Sarah and Kelli waved and Roy and Jeremy returned the gesture. Roy looked at Kelli and thought back to those months of his wife's pregnancy and their child's birth. The depths of anguish originate on the cliff from which you fall, and none as great as the loss of a child. Life was good, and then the steep plunge. "No more," she said, the emotional pain too great, the fall too deep. She would never bear a child again. Time and distance helped ease the pain for Roy, but not Sarah. The garden was her memorial, the daily reminders too raw. *She could be my granddaughter*, Roy thought as the Stearman lumbered toward the far end of the farm.

Jeremy's leather skullcap and headphones fit comfortably snug. They were familiar, a curtain between ear and engine, making the Lycoming's roar distant and less of a distraction. It was all he could hear until Roy spoke to him.

"You taxi slow," Roy said. "No faster than a fat man's jog. If you taxi too fast, then turn, the momentum can swing you around and cause a wingtip to dig into the ground. Bad, real bad."

"I can't see what's in front of me," Jeremy said.

"I know, just get a feel for the speed."

"Didn't we take off the other way the last time?"

"Yep, we did. Look at the weather vane on the barn, and the leaves atop the trees. What do you see?"

Jeremy noticed the rusted red metal rooster sitting on an arrow, the four points of the compass just below its feet. "North, the wind's from the north."

"Good. And the trees?" Roy asked.

"What about them?"

"Do their leaves match the weather vane?"

"Match?"

"Move in the same direction."

"Yes," Jeremy said.

"And the small branches at their tips, are they moving?"

"No." Jeremy remembered their first flight and Roy's words came back to him. *What do your eyes see that the world already knows? Be open to it and it will reveal itself.*

"Correct. That means the winds are about six miles per hour. If the branches were moving, six to twelve miles per hour. We take off into the wind."

"Why?"

"Because those six miles per hour are six less we have to accelerate to fly," Roy said.

"More wind over the wing."

"That's right. More lift and less take-off distance. You gotta use everything that nature gives you."

They taxied to the far end of the farm and Roy turned the Stearman. For Jeremy, the promise of flying was even more portentous and inviting than the last time. They had done this before. It could be done, would be done, on earth as it is in the heavens.

"Control check," Roy said. "Get on the controls with me. Right hand on the stick. Rest your right elbow on the top of your knee." Roy pushed the stick toward his left knee. "Now look outside at the left lower wing,"

Jeremy saw a section stretching the length of the back of the wing move like a door hinged to a door frame. "That's the aileron. Left stick, left up." Jeremy watched the left aileron extend upward. "Right stick, right up," Roy said as he pushed the stick right and Jeremy saw the aileron on the right wing extend upward.

"Look at the wing mirror," Roy said. Jeremy saw Roy and a section of the tail in the small circular mirror. "Stick back, elevator up. Stick forward, elevator down. Got it?"

"Got it," Jeremy said.

"Feet. Right foot, right rudder, left foot, left rudder," Roy said. With every movement, the tail responded with a wave.

"Now you do it," Roy said. "It's the only way to learn." Jeremy took hold of the yoke and operated the controls, watching to see whether the machine would behave as instructed. He was surprised, not that they moved, but that they did so with as little effort as turning his bicycle. The plane was now not only an extension of his hands and legs but his will as well.

"Cool!" Jeremy said.

"It ain't magic and it ain't a dream, kid. Attention to detail. Engine run-up. Inside. Bottom row. Second from right. Temperature gauge. Got it?" Roy asked. Jeremy looked and saw the gauge marked TEMP °C, its dial on forty.

"Got it," Jeremy said.

"The engine has to be at least forty degrees Celsius. If not, you have to wait until the engine warms up."

"Got it."

"Good. Now put your feet firmly on the rudder pedals. Press the

153

tops of the pedals forward. Tops are brakes; the bottom of the pedals control the rudder and the small tail wheel so you can taxi."

Jeremy pressed on the top of the pedals and could feel the resistance of the hydraulic cylinders pushing fluid to the main wheels.

"It's like the tractor," Jeremy said. "Like my bike."

"They're all related in some way. And how's my—I mean your—bicycle working out?"

"Excellent. It's a great ride. And I'd like to try your—"

"Nobody drives my car," Roy said.

"I was thinking the jeep."

"You must be a pilot, always wanting free stuff. We'll discuss that later. Back to business. Bottom right. RPM gauge. Got it?"

"Got it."

"Hold the brakes, bring up the throttle until the RPM gauge reaches 1,500."

"Got it," Jeremy said. He slowly pushed the throttle forward with his left hand and felt the power of the Lycoming engine enter through his fingers and travel through the rest of his body as if it were being possessed. It was not as obedient as the flight controls. It seemed to have a mind of its own, an attitude of its own, the gauge a poor interpreter of its intent. The Stearman wanted to jump and lurch, as if to rip itself away from the bad intentions of the Lycoming engine. Roy took over the controls as he saw Jeremy's wide-eyed expression.

"I got it," Roy said.

"You got it! Take it!" Jeremy said.

"This engine is a whole lotta nasty. But you gotta control it and not let it control you." Roy finished the engine run-up, cycled the propeller, and set the trim for takeoff. Roy knew that too much instruction would overwhelm the best of students. He gave a thumbs-up into the wing mirror and Jeremy tentatively returned the gesture.

"Here we go. Ride the controls with me." Roy pushed the throttle forward and, with the demeanor of a chef explaining step-by-step how to braise a pork shoulder, described the transition from earth to sky. The Stearman rumbled, the earth shook, and the welcoming sky was suspect. *Who is this who wants to be among us?* it asked. There were a dozen distractions and sensory overload, yet Jeremy's focus was on Roy's voice and his instructions. He struggled to keep up, but everyone scuffles in the beginning.

With every instruction by Roy, an observation and thought by Jeremy:

"I'll set 2,200 on the RPM with the throttle," Roy said. *Take-off power.*

"I release the brakes." *He slides his feet down from the brakes. We're moving.*

"A little right rudder keeps us in the middle of the runway." *Rudder is the steering wheel on the ground.*

"The airspeed indicator is off the peg." *Airspeed dial is moving above twenty and increasing. Thirty, forty, and we're moving faster.*

"The control yoke centers because there's enough wind over the tail's elevator." *Wind over the wings like my hand outside the car window.*

"Forty knots the tail lifts and will fly before the main wing, but we're still on the ground." *Forty on the indicator, the tail rises and I can see in front of me.*

"Sixty knots, I pull back on the yoke and break free of the ground." *Sixty on the airspeed dial, the yoke moves back, and we're in the air!*

The Stearman accelerated, the Lycoming engine growled, and Jeremy scuffled to keep up—a fight that he welcomed. No low IQ here. He felt Roy's hands and feet purposefully moving the stick, pedals, and throttle, translating the demands of earth, sky, and machine. *Jugglers use less body parts. Flight demands more.* Jeremy tried to absorb Roy's instructions but was "behind the plane" as the Great South Bay passed beneath them. Roy saw Jeremy's mix of youthful zeal and frustration.

"Everyone scuffles in the beginning," Roy said. "Nobody's born a pilot. Today's lesson is straight and level."

"Yes, sir."

"Pitch, power, and airspeed. They're all connected. Let's start with pitch. Where does the horizon cut through your windscreen?"

Jeremy pondered the question for a few seconds. The horizon expanded beyond the view of the diminutive screen deflecting the wind.

"The horizon cuts through the windshield from left to right," Jeremy said.

"Language. Get it right. It's a windscreen, not a windshield. What part of the windscreen?"

"The bottom."

"Divide the windscreen into thirds. Which third?"

"Last third," Jeremy answered.

"Top, middle, or bottom?"

"Bottom third."

"Good. Step two: where is the nose of the aircraft?"

"I can't see the nose."

"The part you *can* see," Roy asked. "You can see the top, can't ya?"

"Yes. It's slightly above the horizon."

"Good. You place the horizon level on the bottom third of the windscreen and dial it in with the nose slightly above it. That's the correct pitch, the correct attitude for level flight from the front seat. Got it?"

"Attitude?" Jeremy asked

"Excellent. You're listening. Attention to detail. Attitude not altitude. One will give you the other with the correct power setting. Both are related but different," Roy said.

"Got it. And from the back?" Jeremy asked.

"It's a different sight picture. You're thinking correctly, but don't get ahead of yourself. One control at a time. Feet on the floor. Left hand on your lap. Right hand on the yoke."

"Level flight?"

"Correct. You have the yoke."

The yoke was no thicker than a broomstick handle, and Jeremy squeezed the black plastic grip covering the painted metal end. The horizon filled the bottom third of the windscreen, the nose slightly above it. As advertised. The Stearman was "connected" to the distant horizon a hundred miles away. How, he didn't know, but he had to trust, had to believe that everything was connected in some way. Jeremy muscle-locked the yoke in place as it was handed to him.

"Level flight," said Roy. "You want proof. Look at the climb indicator."

Jeremy glanced at the gauge scribed climb. The dial was parallel with the horizon and pointed to zero. The numbers above and below mirrored each other. Up five, down five. The horizon, windscreen, aircraft's nose, and the gauge were linked. *Level flight. Math.*

"Stir the yoke a little bit and get a feel for the airplane," Roy said.

Jeremy moved the yoke and the ailerons traveled on their hinges. The resistance of wind on the yoke was like that of Jeremy's hand outside the window of his grandfather's car at highway speed. The Stearman slowly listed to the right.

"Level flight," Roy said. "Bring it back left. Get that picture back in the windscreen."

"Okay," Jeremy said. He overcorrected and the Stearman banked left and then to the right again. The right wing lowered, the left wing rose, and the picture in the windscreen was gone as if stolen from a museum. The ocean filled the windscreen, the nose wanting to part the waves. Jeremy looked at the climb indicator and it pointed down. The cockpit dials scurried in every direction like a pile of garter snakes roiling out of their nest. All was disconnected.

"You got it!" Jeremy said.

"Nope," Roy said. "Remember the procedure."

"Okay, okay, okay—" Jeremy said, his voice rising.

"Okay. Then do something," Roy said calmly as the ocean loomed larger. Jeremy pulled back on the yoke, the weight of his inexperience pressing him into the seat. The horizon slowly came into view as he placed it level in the bottom third of the windscreen and the nose of the Stearman slightly above. He remembered. The gauges calmed and the climb indicator pointed to zero, the stolen picture returned to its rightful place in the museum. Jeremy smiled.

"Good," Roy said. "Good." The same invisible antiseptic air that Jeremy choked on in juvenile hall was the same air that kept the Stearman afloat, its wooden propeller slicing through it and pulling them forward. *Amazing.*

"Relax," Roy said. "It's all about small adjustments and anticipating what the aircraft is going to do. That will come with time. With every turn is a decrease in lift. A little back pressure on the yoke and a slight increase in power and we won't be swimming with the fishes."

Jeremy trusted, and level flight now became level turns.

"Left hand on the throttle. Pitch, now power," Roy said.

Jeremy wrapped his left hand around the throttle and could feel the Lycoming's infernal combustion and hear its guttural growl. He wondered who had whom by the throat.

"Power. The RPM gauge on the bottom right. Got it?" Roy asked.

Jeremy moved his eyes from outside the airplane to the cockpit's panel. "Got it."

"Excellent. Set the gauge to fourteen. That's 1,400 RPM," Roy said.

With his left hand Jeremy tentatively advanced the throttle and the RPM needle moved upward. The Lycoming engine complied, the wooden propeller quickened, and the biplane's wings surfed the viscous air. Pitch. Power. Airspeed. Everything is connected. Change the pitch, change the power, and both affect the airspeed. They followed each other, and Jeremy felt all three through his senses, the Stearman's gauges quantifying the invisible. *Math.*

He trusted the wisdom and experience of the old man. *Let the plane speak to you through the controls*—and like the tractor, it eventually did. Jeremy relaxed his grip and correctly remembered the procedures that Roy had taught. Through all the distractions his concentration became more focused yet expansive, this just one of the many contradictions of flight, its very nature a contradiction. His consciousness had to jump from horizon to gauge to hands and back again, his body a barometer of his actions. Flight demanded attention, constant attention, his mind wanting to take in the view, the poetry of it all, its surreal magic of it all. But this wasn't a dream, it was now an extension of his will, expressed through the limits of this magnificent machine.

What it wasn't was a psychologist or an "expert" from family services telling him what he was not or could never be. It was life telling him what he could be if he tried, if he was engaged. Through luck and good fortune he now wanted to be something. To reach, to try, to want, knowing that failure or success wasn't the goal, but his own salvation.

"That's enough for one day," Roy said. "You did well, Jeremy. Let's go home."

Jeremy banked the plane, knowing the way.

CHAPTER 4

galileo's notebook

LIKE CLOCKWORK, after every school day Jeremy and Kelli rode up the dusty dirt road and arrived at the farm. It was not out of obligation or to escape the world. No longer children, they understood, more so than most teenagers their age, the complicated and confusing world that they lived in. The farm was a place that affirmed the goodness of the world. And without fail, they left buoyed in mind and spirit at the end of each day, leaving with a bit of knowledge and wisdom that only those who live off the land could bestow.

Meanwhile, Jeremy was excelling at school. Moved by his voracious appetite for knowledge fueled by the teachings of flight, he completed modules on a pace with Kelli. He arrived at school early and scoured the internet for topics Roy introduced to him. On those subjects that he wanted to dig deeper, he explored at the local public library. There he found books of all sizes and weights, and the heft of their knowledge was not a weapon but a gift.

Jeremy also excelled at flying, the Stearman and the tangible act of flight bridging him to the academic world. Flying required not only science but also the humanities and many other subject areas. Why and how became his favorite words and a call to knowledge.

Jeremy's enthusiasm had also reawakened Roy's passion for life, his world becoming a bit brighter and a little less sepia. And on those days when the weather didn't cooperate or Kelli's morning sickness kept her home, Roy taught with the perspective of a historian and the knowledge of a science teacher.

"Before airplanes there were the great sailing ships from as far back as the 1400s," Roy said. "Those brave men and the knowledge they accrued are the building blocks passed on to us. The birth of flight started at sea and touches on many subjects. You don't need to be an expert, but you must have a working knowledge of the fields of study that influence flight."

When they next flew, sailboats took on a different meaning, one no longer of envy but of interest. Jeremy recalled those countless long summer days perched on his tree in the sand, watching fathers at the tillers of their sailboats with beers in hand and family members lounging on the boats' decks, eating and laughing with not a care in the world. *Why are they the keeper of the wind? And why is there no room for me?* Jeremy had once asked. No more.

Looking down from the Stearman's cockpit, Jeremy saw sailboats upon the bay, their unfurled sails catching the wind. The sails were wings turned up on end, harnessing the breeze and propelling the sailboats forward. Like the weather vane pointing its nose into the wind, both the sailboats and Stearman harnessed the power of nature. The Old World and New World explorers were now one. Flying past the lighthouse at Montauk Point, this was never more apparent, with Roy teaching the skills of navigating by reference to fixed points on the earth and using much of the language and knowledge learned five hundred years past. Knots. Nautical miles. Statute miles, bearing. Compass, rudder, true course, magnetic course.

A breath of fresh ocean air swayed the long reed grass and cooled his castle by the sea. Why is there wind? What causes it? How do those clouds stay aloft in the blue sky? A child's question, but a young boy's quest to know. The wings of fabric and the mainsails of cloth, subjugated to the will of Mother Nature.

"You're drifting. Correct for it. You got legs—use them. You can't fly this plane without the rudder. Feet, young man. Aileron and rudder. Gotta lean into it. Redirect the ship!" Roy said, the lighthouse quickly moving away as Jeremy tried to circle the landmark.

Jeremy corrected for the wind, nature indifferent to his intentions. Like the seafaring captains suffering the toils of nature, Jeremy experienced turbulence, and it felt no different than hitting a pothole with the front wheel of his bicycle.

He returned to earth with a desire to know the whys of wind and turbulence. The world of meteorology, he would find, is as much of a mystery as science. And in his quest for answers each discovery fed into another question and another field of study. His composition book from his days in middle school, its cover patterned in black-and-white marble, no longer gathered dust in a forgotten corner of his bedroom. Its binding of thread and tape barely held together the never-ending knowledge he scribed into its paltry one hundred pages.

Discovery became a feast of steak and potatoes, macaroni and cheese not included. He wrote in his once-empty composition book: As Galileo studied the stars I study the sky and earth! I will make notes in my notebook as he did in his:

- The world has a magnetic field generated from molten, liquid metal surrounding the earth's core that powers the Stearman's compass.
- The earth rotates around a single axis, the Stearman around three and the tilt of the earth causes the change in seasons.
- The fury of the Lycoming engine is fueled by minuscule sea creatures and an array of shells the planet's inner heat cooked into oil over the millenniums. I understand why it

is called fossil fuel.

- The world isn't round as I thought. Oblate spheroid. The world has a waistline.

- The sky is blue, space black, and the sunset red. Why? The sky is blue because the atmosphere scatters the blue light. Space is black because there is no atmosphere to scatter the light. And the sunset is red because the longer wavelength of red reaches the eye.

- Lightening is not caused by comic book characters or Greek gods but by negative charged clouds and the positive earth below. Water droplets and ice crystals connect earth and sky; a bolt of lightning is four times hotter than the surface of the sun and width no wider than a half dollar. Cool!

- Both the ocean and air are fluids conforming to the same set of mathematical principles. A dolphin essentially flies through the sea and a seagull swims through the air.

- Daniel Bernoulli. An increase in speed is a decrease in pressure; the dolphin is seagull, the submarine is airplane. All is connected.

- I see the whitecaps break atop the waves on the bay's surface and wonder how the wind carries my voice through the air. Through my headset, electromagnetic waves, radio waves, carry my voice and those I hear at the speed of light! My voice, at the speed of light, crests and troughs like that of the oceans. Never once until now did I question how mom's cell phone worked, the computer at school or a car radio. My interest as limited as visible light to the human eye.

- My voice transmitted at the speed of light. Radio: James Clerk Maxwell. Heinrich Hertz, Guglielmo Marconi, Edouard Branly, the greats of the invisible voice.

- Who are the great minds that figure this out! It's not one but many. Discovery is built of sheer determination. The unearthing of knowledge by one is built on by others and the boulder is slowly muscled up Innovation Mountain. Men and women many who probably never met and all are connected!

- Newton will take the torch from Galileo as all others in literature from Shakespeare.

- It started with a small toy of bamboo, cork and paper, a gift to Orville and Wilbur Wright by their father. A rubber band powers the small, fragile, helicopter's blades. It breaks and they fix it. The beginning. ~~My father gave me nothing~~. My father gave me life. I give myself opportunity!

- Why do boats sink and clouds float? Mass and density. Clouds float because the water molecules (mass) that make up the cloud are spread out and less dense than the air around it. The *Stranger* floats because it displaces a huge amount of water that weighs more than the ferry. Its total density is less than the water around it and it floats. When it leaks the reverse and it sinks. Cool!

- An imaginary grid covers the earth. It looks like a fence but this fence doesn't keep me out. Latitude and longitude. Measurements in degrees, minutes, and seconds and I can locate any place in the world! Roy showed me how to read an aviation sectional chart and find any place on a globe if I know the coordinates. To navigate using the Stearman's whiskey compass and comparing what I see from the air to what's on the chart. It is the X and Y of a math graph paper coming to life! The chart means something!

- Changing gears. Going uphill. First gear moves you a shorter distance for each spin of the bicycle pedals because the gear is smaller. That makes it "easier" to pedal because less distance is less energy. Now going downhill, second or third gear, moves you farther with each spin of the pedals. The gears are larger, and it's "harder" to move the wheel that greater distance with one stroke than it does to move it a shorter distance with more strokes. Now I know! Cool!

CHAPTER 5

roots

IT TOOK ROOT. It took root as his anger left him and was replaced by knowledge. It took root when intelligent discourse replaced his sullen silence. It took root as passion replaced indifference. It took root as his youthful emotional affect grew into the persona of an honorable young man.

Her mind and body at war, Kelli's attraction took root. She could no longer dismiss her flushed skin or the butterflies in her stomach as an effect of pregnancy. She had never felt more beautiful, never more despised: the looks in public, the scorn toward someone so young and so pregnant, her belly a scarlet letter. But not to Jeremy, and to her that was all that mattered. And when he shoved his tongue into her mouth it wasn't a tease but intent, an intent she bathed in. For Jeremy it was another dimension of Kelli to explore. Her tongue, her taste, her smell to be shared in as well as her mind. To revel in the joys of teenage love.

He never thought the benefits of learning would lead to this, yet here they were.

CHAPTER 6

ODD

THE PRINCIPAL OF FRONTIER and his minions stood anxiously at the curb as they watched Mrs. Carol Morgan Spring arrive in her white Mercedes coupe, prepared to treat her like a head of state.

The half-day "parent"/teacher conference was mandatory. It was a rare sight to see both biological parents, and a better description would have been a guardian/teacher conference. Grandparents, aunts, uncles, and legal guardians from a host of tangled relationships attended the conference along with many single moms. Few fathers ever showed.

Carol was the legal guardian of Kelli and eight other girls, and her guardianship was given the full attention of the school's principal and staff. It didn't hurt that, outside federal and state funding, she was the largest contributor to the school. She also had a direct hand in creating a curriculum that reflected the needs of her pregnant wards.

Collins didn't run his conferences like most teachers. He insisted that the parent/guardian read his notes before their face-to-face meeting, and in the very seat where their child sat, this in full view of the parents for the upcoming meetings, which he invariably started at least fifteen minutes late. He was a man supremely confident in the privileges and protections afforded him by the teachers' union.

He lectured his captive audience like a college professor, denouncing anything they might have to say and smirking at their discomfort. All the while, he spoke in a loosely British accent despite the fact that he had never traveled overseas.

Clare took in the view of the windowless room, sat in Jeremy's seat, and read her son's progress report.

> *Student Effort and Academic Progress*: Jeremy's effort his first five weeks was one of abject indifference. He completed none of his assignments and was told in no uncertain terms he was in jeopardy of being expelled from the school. I am suspect of his sudden turn toward academic progress. In short, I believe he is cheating.
>
> *Student Behavior and Social Skills:* Academic assistance from other students is prohibited in class. Conversation is also frowned upon. Jeremy violates both rules. I believe he's in cahoots with one particular student and has been told to cease and desist. Their "friendship" and his sudden academic progress are suspiciously coincidental.
>
> Without exception every conversation we've had has been confrontational. He is without remorse for his behavior in class and the cause of his being at Frontier. At times I worry about my own safety. Rumor has it he has a nickname and relishes in its connotation. Violence seems to simmer beneath the surface of his every action.
>
> *Teacher Recommendations*: I believe Jeremy is hyperactive, has difficulty paying attention, and is impulsive. I've instructed the school guidance counselor along with the school psychologist to perform a full psychological and academic assessment. Additionally, I recommend his New York State Juvenile Psychiatric Evaluation be reviewed prior to the new workup. It states and I agree with the findings of weekly

professional counseling and medication. Most importantly medication. Many of my students are on Adderall, Dexedrine, and Ritalin, to name a few. After two or three weeks I've noticed their comportment is within the norms of acceptable behavior. Frontier will administer, at no cost to the parent, the counseling and medicine during normal school hours at the nurse's office.

Parents Questions and Concerns (Complete during the conference)

Clare finished reading and sat in silence, every word another cut. Death by a thousand cuts. She bled guilt and disappointment like only a parent could. This was not the child she imagined, this was not the child she knew, but if this was what the teacher said, it must be true. She waited her turn, waiting and wondering, bleeding.

◆ ◆ ◆

With Kelli still in the throes of morning sickness and Clare attending the parent/teacher conference at Frontier, Jeremy looked forward to a full day on the tractor bush-hogging the fescue grass. He arrived to see the Wednesday regulars of the One of Us club, who welcomed him warmly.

"Breakfast for the boy!" Betty said.

"He's cutting into my bacon quota," Gus said. "And maybe he's eaten already."

"He's a growing boy, Gus," Betty said. "Feed him."

Jeremy sat at the end of the table as Gus brought him breakfast. "No wind, clear skies. Nice day to fly," the old man said. "You'll do fine son, but just in case—" He took out a small vial of water from his pocket. "Holy water. Do you mind?"

"You're scaring the kid," Dixon said. "He don't need a cleansing—you do!"

Jeremy devoured his delicious breakfast, far more interested in the last bite of his applewood-smoked bacon than the sign of the cross and the holy water Gus sprinkled on him.

"Don't mind them, Jeremy, they're all one wave short of a shipwreck," Betty said.

Jeremy smiled as Roy looked at him and pointed to the jeep.

"Let's go, young man," Roy said.

"I was going to—"

"No hogging today."

"Cool. Can I—"

"Nope. I drive," Roy said. They jumped into the jeep and drove to the far end of the field. At farm's end Roy turned the jeep around, backing it up against a tree and shutting off the engine.

"Look up," Roy said. "How high are the trees?"

"Fifty feet?"

"Close. Sixty. Look toward the far end of the farm. How far is it?"

"I have no idea," Jeremy said.

"Guess."

"Two miles?"

"No. Three-quarters of a mile," Roy said. "My grandfather wanted two but could only afford one. My father sold some acreage years back. How long is a mile?"

"Five thousand, two hundred eighty feet minus 1,760 feet is . . . about 3,500 feet."

"Not bad."

Jeremy smiled. "Turns out I'm good at math. Who would have thought?"

"Close—it's 3,520. Don't give up the twenty. Never give up real estate. And the height of the trees on the far end?"

"Sixty feet."

"Nope, seventy. Back in the jeep." Roy drove a few hundred feet and stopped at what Jeremy found to be an unusual place on the field. He shut off the engine and walked to the back of the vehicle. "Extend your arm, point to the tree line," Roy said.

Jeremy extended his right arm and pointed to the tree they were sitting under just a few moments ago.

"Now put your chin on your shoulder so your eye line follows your arm."

Jeremy did so, and Roy nudged Jeremy's arm up above the tree line.

"You see that?" Roy asked.

"See what? I'm pointing at the sky."

"True, but more precisely a specific spot in the sky. That's eighty-five feet, twenty-five feet above the trees at a three-degree angle. Got it?"

"Got it," Jeremy said.

"No you don't." Roy pushed Jeremy's extended arm toward the ground. "Threshold, beginning of the grass runway. Imagine a slide from that point in the sky to the spot beneath your feet."

"A slide?"

"Yeah, a slide like into a pool or at the playground. From that point in the air to this point beneath your feet." Roy reached into the jeep, pulled out a can of white spray paint, and sprayed two ten-foot lines on the ground on either side of the jeep.

"And if I can't hit this spot?" Jeremy asked.

"In the jeep," Roy said as he tossed him the can of spray paint.

◆ ◆ ◆

From his desk Collins invited Clare, in his newfound quasi-British accent, to come forward as if she were not a parent or even a student but a defendant about to be addressed by a barrister in some magistrate's court. She walked timidly to the front of the room, her feeling of dread heightened as she approached, and sat at a student's desk that he'd set up in front of his.

"I believe your son has ADHD and would benefit from medication," Collins said.

"He's never been on any—"

"And that's why you'd see improved behavior that would lead to better grades."

"But he's—"

"He's an angry young boy entering manhood. That's a dangerous thing. You did read my evaluation report? You do know how to read, don't you?"

"I do!" Clare said, her anger simmering.

"It must be tough being a single mom incapable of filling the role of a man. No balance in the kid's life."

"Incapable?"

"Facts are facts. Just as I can't fill the role of a mother, you can't fill the role of a father. Protector, provider, counselor. Defender of the home, primary breadwinner, a man's reasoned opinion and shared sacrifice in raising a family. You son simply did not experience this. How old are you?"

"Thirty," she said.

"And you son is fourteen."

"Yes, I was sixteen."

"That's a common story around here. Fathers leave for a . . . reason," he said.

Clare simmered, too angry to respond.

"It's my job not only to educate but to evaluate," Collins continued. "You do want him to graduate?"

"Of course I do!" she said.

"Then I think medication is the best thing for him. You'd be negligent if you didn't cooperate."

"He's not a violent boy. We—"

"Funny you say that. It's the only prerequisite to get into this fine institution. No mother thinks of her—"

"Mr. Collins—"

"Please don't interrupt me," he said.

"Interrupt?! That's all you've done!"

"He's one mistake away from prison."

"Aren't we all!"

"I can see where he gets his ODD!"

"ODD?"

"Yes, oppositional defiant disorder."

"Another diagnosis?" she said in frustration.

"Correct. And your behavior explains his attraction to Kelli. She must remind him of you. She's the wrong type of girl but he's safe—for at least the next few months, at least. It's just a matter of time before—"

"Enough!" A voice boomed from the door of the school trailer, practically knocking them out of their chairs. It could have awoken the dead. Carol, unnoticed, had been standing there and listening to it all.

◆ ◆ ◆

Roy stopped his jeep in the middle of the field. Again he shut the engine and walked to the back of the vehicle with Jeremy following. Roy sprayed another two lines on either side of the jeep.

"This marks the end of the first third of the grass runway," Roy said. "It's not a spot but an area, a touchdown zone. Landing on the first third of the field is the mark of a true professional. Remember what I said about humility. You're learning. You never want to give up real estate, but if you can't make your mark that's okay. Back in the jeep, kid."

They drove about another thousand feet, Roy's eyes looking at the top of the tree line at the far end of the farm. He stopped again and sprayed another set of lines. "These ones are the most important," he said.

"Why?"

"Look at the trees and answer your question."

Jeremy looked at the trees, the sprayed lines, and then Roy.

"If I don't have it on the ground by here, time to go around."

"Correct. No ifs, ands, or buts. This line is the end of the second third of the field. Some landings go long. A gust of wind, you're too fast, whatever the reason, if you don't have the plane on the ground and under control by this line, you must go around. Do you understand?"

"Yes, sir."

"You never want to be in the last third of the field trying to figure out what to do. By then it's too late. You won't clear the trees. Understood?"

"Yes, sir," Jeremy said again.

"And how do you go around?"

"Pitch, power, airspeed."

"Correct. Full power while you simultaneously pitch for a nose up attitude. You'll get your airspeed back pretty quickly. The Continental engine may be small, but it has more than enough power. What do you pitch to?"

"Tree line plus twenty-five feet. Continental engine? What's—?"

"Clear the trees. Get over the trees. Twenty feet or more is ideal but over the tree line."

◆ ◆ ◆

"Enough!" Carol said again. She walked toward the front of the room and stood over Collins, who even when he stood up to face her did so only eye to eye. "Your reasoned opinion is garbage!"

"Excuse me?!" Mr. Collins said.

"Excuse nothing! 'Reasoned opinion'?! You lost that with your hairline, if you ever had it to begin with! Shared sacrifice! Dogshit!" she yelled, her elegant manner gone, her anger in full force, this stranger expressing what Clare couldn't.

"You can't touch me!"

"No woman would want to!"

"I have tenure!"

"Tenure doesn't give you the right to speak to a mother, no less a dog, like that!"

"I speak the truth!"

"No! You speak your failings!" Carol thundered. "This place should be about hope!"

"Hope? It's about failed parents, failed students, and a failed school system. The only hope is that these kids stay long enough so the school district can get their federal funding. The school district gets its money and the student, ill-prepared for the real world, gets a worthless piece of paper."

"Then help prepare them!"

"I tried!"

"Try harder!"

"Easy for you to say," Collins sneered. "Try teaching kids who come here hungry and without sleep. The ills of society don't stop at the school fence."

"Then show what society can be. Don't take it out on her!" Carol said, pointing to Clare in her front-row seat to the warring parties, a war she was realizing had begun well before today.

"Hit too close to home, Mrs. Spring?" Collins said in his quasi-British accent. "A teenage single parent yourself, trying to make up for that lost son? How many girls this year, eight? Try ten next semester, maybe that will ease your pain."

"My pain would have put a weak man like you six feet under a long time ago. But this is not about me! This is about these children! These kids are more than the wrongs they committed!"

"I've done my job and given my best advice!"

"Ridicule, suspicion, derision, and then top it off with medication! Please! Where's your proof that Jeremy's cheating?"

"I'm not at liberty to tell you!"

"Then tell me," Clare said tentatively as she looked up at this stranger defending her, this person she'd never met, a guardian of eight girls. Eight! She stood, looking at Mr. Collins and, if only for a fleeting moment, said without timidity, "Yes, please tell me!"

◆ ◆ ◆

It stood out like a field of yellow dandelions, a yellow hue at first reminding Jeremy of the dreaded school bus with the black bird painted above its door. As they approached the farmhouse it glowed even brighter, its black streak not a bird but a lightning bolt. The One of Us club sat comfortably in picnic chairs beside the yellow aircraft awaiting their return.

It was slightly longer than a car, weighed thousands less, and its fuselage was as wide as Jeremy was slender. It stood as tall as Jeremy was short, had only one set of wings, and its tires were cartoonishly small. Jeremy stepped out of the jeep and carefully inspected the tiny plane of fabric and metal. He looked inside the sparse cockpit to witness the definition of economy: a throttle, a yoke, a few instruments, and little else. A small metal placard with five simple words was riveted beneath the altimeter. *Rear seat for solo flight.* Jeremy read it silently, grinned, and walked clockwise toward the tail. On the rudder was a decal of a little bear cub holding a sign: PIPER CUB. *This must be a model, a fake, not the real thing.*

At the front of the Cub, the propeller looked more like a fan, its size more appropriate for the kitchen table in his apartment. The engine was small, motorcycle small, with sixty-five horses. Its pistons stuck out like a kid with a wad of gum in his cheeks. The Stearman's eight-piston radial engine was big and stout, its power equal to its furious roar; the Cub's four-cylinder engine, flat and barely visible, seemed almost like an afterthought. Jeremy couldn't see how it could be a match for the bind of gravity. Pushing gently on the strut that connected the wing of wood and fabric to the fuselage, he moved the plane with less effort than he would his bicycle.

"Don't kid yourself, it flies," Dixon said.

"That it does," Gus said. "We chipped in and bought it together. For years we'd go flying after breakfast."

"Now we just eat," Dixon said.

"And talk, don't forget about talking," Cliff said.

"And pee," Lewis said.

"And sh—" Cliff said.

"The kid gets it, Cliff," Betty said.

"Hasn't flown in a while, like most of us," Dixon said. "It's meant to be up there, not on the ground."

"We figure you're all right with Roy, you're all right with us," Lewis said.

"All of you are—" Jeremy asked.

"Yes," Betty said. "Roy taught us all."

"Yes, even her," Cliff said.

"Thanks for the compliment, dickweed," Betty said.

"She's the best of the group, smooth pilot," Roy said. A collective groan went up among the old men.

"Extra bacon for you next Wednesday," Betty said to Roy.

Jeremy looked at all of them, into their ageless eyes, and it had been there all along, he just hadn't seen it until now.

"Roy," Jeremy said.

"Yeah?"

"Which seat?"

"The front one. You do know how to read, don't ya?"

"Yeah, but that back seat looks pretty small."

"Let me worry about that," Roy said. "Let's go flying."

"Let's," Jeremy said, and the group roared its approval.

◆　◆　◆

The principal had finally separated the warring parties. He cringed outside the trailer next to Clare and Carol as the two women introduced each other.

"I'm Mrs. Carol Morgan Spring. My apologies for intervening in such a forceful manner. I could have handled that in a more diplomatic way."

"None needed. I'm Clare."

"Clare. Beautiful name. And your last name?"

"McNeal."

"Middle name?"

"Darcy."

"Ms. Clare Darcy McNeal. Now that's befitting. A beautiful name for a beautiful young lady," Carol said in her distinguished, melodic voice. It was the first time in Clare's adult life that anyone outside the state unemployment agency or the police sergeant at the Fifth Precinct had called Clare by her full name. For as long as she could remember, she had felt it was a source of embarrassment. "You've sullied our good family name," her father had said as he kicked his teenage daughter out of his house. It was a heretofore forgotten pleasure to hear her name spoken free of insinuation.

"Thank you," Clare said.

"I've met your son. He's none of those things. Don't believe a word of it."

"None of it? How can you be so sure?"

"Cause I know my Red," Carol said.

"My who?"

"My Kelli; I'm her legal guardian, though I hate that term. She's my daughter. She's spoken highly of your Jeremy and he's been a guest at my home. Well-mannered, respectful, and most importantly he's searching to find his way. That's all you can ask of a child. We all make mistakes, it's only fools who make these young kids constantly pay for them," she said, tossing her head at the principal.

"I have six other conferences to attend," Carol added, "but we must talk again." Then she gave Clare an unsolicited hug. The floral scent of her perfume, the softness of her fine clothes, and the warmth of her embrace reminded Clare of her own mother when times were different, when times were good. Clare held on longer than appropriate, closing her eyes and taking in her spirit, her iron will, her love.

◆　◆　◆

The numbers astonished Jeremy. With a full tank of gas (nine gallons), the Cub could reach Boston from Long Island 160 miles away and no farther. Its top speed couldn't match cars on the Long Island Expressway, and it could land on a piece of real estate smaller than a football field at a gravity defying thirty-eight miles per hour. A tail-wheeled airplane with its nose steeply pointed upward, it had little in common with the stalwart Stearman.

"Enough talk, time to fly," Roy said. He looked at the small confines of the back seat of the Piper Cub, exhaled, and, to the amusement of the seniors watching, bumped his head on the wooden wing as he snaked his arthritic six-foot-two body into the rear seat of the fabric-covered tubular steel fuselage. "Five pounds of shit in a four pound bag," he grumbled to the laughter of the crowd.

Jeremy jumped into the front seat. A perfect fit. Stick, throttle, rudder pedals all within his reach. Gus stood in front of the propeller and he pulled the prop through when Roy gave him the sign. It started with ease and didn't growl, spit, nor roar in furious contempt like the Stearman. The cockpit filled with a blast of air thick with the smell of gasoline, oil, and grass. It was as if the Cub was welcoming Jeremy and Roy.

Jeremy taxied to the far end of the field with the touch and skill developed in the many hours flying the Stearman. He ran the engine checks and returned the throttle to idle. Roy reminded Jeremy during the take-off roll to use his feet and his peripheral vision to stay aligned with the grass runway. Jeremy smoothly advanced the throttle, and the fresh breeze of acceleration filled the cockpit. He tapped on the right rudder pedal, keeping the Cub pointed straight, his line of sight blocked by the Cub's nose.

The Cub's tail gently lifted and its wing took hold of the viscous air. He eased back on the stick and the plane gently rose above the ground after only a few hundred feet. It climbed easily at fifty-five miles per hour, quickly outpaced by the westbound train heading for New York City below. They turned out toward the bay a stone's throw above the ground and Jeremy was amazed. In its simplicity was its attraction, in its ease to fly its purity. In its seventy years of flight a storied history, a living history that Jeremy was now connected to. He performed steep turns, climbed, and descended. All with ease, all spot on. The Cub was stable, the controls well-balanced, and it righted itself each time. It inhabited both sky and earth with ease. It did not conquer either but was in harmony with both. Jeremy was convinced that this machine was built by the hand of man but guided by the spirit of the aviation gods.

The ocean air's salty scent that filled the cockpit was pure—embryonic, because we are all made of the sea.

"Time to go home," Roy said.

"Yes, sir," a reluctant Jeremy said. "Thanks, Roy."

"Thank the group. It was their idea."

"I'll start with you," Jeremy said, bringing his left hand over his left shoulder. Roy reached out and shook it.

"We're not done yet."

They flew over the farm, the right wing paralleling property's end six hundred feet below, and Jeremy saw the sprayed white lines delineating the grass runway. Roy rode the controls with Jeremy and talked him through the first landing. Not a wasted word, not a "please" or "try to," his instruction sparse yet precise: "Throttle to idle. Carburetor heat on. Stick forward. Normal glide."

What made the Cub easy to fly made it a challenge to land at first. It was light and subject to the whims of the wind as it passed below the tree line. Its nose sat high and the view forward disappeared just when you wanted to see it most. You had to slow down, way down, and trust in Bernoulli and that the Cub's magnificent outstretched wing would outwrestle Newton. Fly or fall. At the hands of a properly trained pilot the Cub could glide one hundred feet for every ten feet of altitude loss. But you must slow down. Way down.

A descending turn and Roy idled the engine; it purred like a sleeping cat, saying "Wake me when we land." They lined up with the grass runway as they descended toward earth. Jeremy was too quick with the control yoke, too much police officer wielding a baton rather than a symphony conductor conducting Mendelssohn's *Calm Sea and Prosperous Voyage.* He increased the throttle only to have Roy return it to idle. He felt a hint, a suggestion, a tap of the controls, an echo telling him that less was more. Trust. Trust. Trust. All is connected.

On his first attempt at landing he bounced hard three times before coming to a full stop, the sprayed white line beneath the Cub's wheels, sniffing the last third of real estate. The next five landings were no better, to the amusement of the seniors watching.

"Tractor," Roy said as they taxied back toward field's end.

"Time for me to bush-hog? You've had enough?"

"Nope. But I do have to pee."

"One more," Jeremy insisted.

"You keep bouncing this thing and my bladder might let loose."

"One more!"

"Okay. One more! Tractor," Roy repeated.

Tractor? Jeremy wondered.

Tractor. He thought back to his first time on the American Harvester. When after many hours of toil and bruises there was a moment his grip on the steering wheel lightened and his feet were no longer a vise on the pedals and when he sat taller in the seat. The moment when his confidence grew into conviction and conviction into trust and with every input the tractor's dutiful response. *Trust yourself, trust Bernoulli, trust the Cub, and trust Roy.* It flew slow, very slow. The airspeed indicator, the green line between fly or fall, at thirty-eight miles an hour. Trust. Kelli's voice resonated once in dream and now in life. *Fly or fall, find your way tonight.*

"Last one, make it count," Roy said.

Turning final on his last approach of the day with the engine at idle and nose slightly down, they passed over the trees at field's edge and descended toward earth. Jeremy was where he was supposed to be on the "pool slide." The Cub slowed below fifty miles per hour as Jeremy aligned its nose with the grass runway and raised the nose. *Throttle. No. Less is more.* He rounded out the flare ten feet above the first set of sprayed lines at thirty-eight miles per hour and turned his head toward the side window. *Flare, side window, thirty-eight. Trust.* His mind quiet and hands serene, he slowly pulled back on the yoke as the Cub slowed and settled.

In that space between fly or fall, Bernoulli or Newton, earth or sky, wing or wheels, plane or tricycle, is one of the many mysteries of flight. It is there where magic and math dance, where dream and reality tango, and it is in that moment where aerodynamic formulas give way to poetic verse and where all description is wanting. The wheels tickled, then kissed the fescue grass, and Jeremy's body warmed to the welcoming earth. All was connected. Trust he had, and the Cub came to rest in just a few hundred feet.

"Now you can cut the grass," Roy said.

"Now you can pee!" Jeremy said. He smiled knowing that in this act of flight he had demonstrated everything that he'd been taught in the many hours flying the Stearman. There was much more to learn, but he had landed an airplane by himself. They taxied back, greeted by the applause of the One of Us club as Lewis rolled his wheelchair up to Jeremy as he exited the Cub.

"The last one. All you?" Lewis asked.

"All me," Jeremy said.

"Congratulations," Lewis said, shaking his hand.

"Thank you."

"Feels good, doesn't it?"

"It does. Like nothing I've ever known."

"Indescribable. I know." Lewis looked at Roy. "Is he ready?"

"Nope," Roy said. "But I've been thinking. How 'bout a Saturday picnic, fresh corn from the garden and some barbeque to welcome the new season? We've haven't had one of those in a long time."

CHAPTER 7

of...

JEREMY WALKED INTO HIS basement apartment to an eerie silence. Clare was sitting on the couch with the television off, staring through the confines of their subterranean walls. Jeremy saw his progress report lying on the coffee table, picked it up, read a few lines, and took a seat beside his mother. He considered whether he should put up a spirited defense against the false, scurrilous picture that Collins had painted. He hardly cared what Collins thought, but his mother's opinion was a different matter. Mom and son, they did not know each other though they thought otherwise, a mystery to be addressed or simply discarded.

She looked away from the wall and into his eyes. A mother knows her son—how could she not? A son his mother, how could he not? Is my son a cheater? Is my mother nothing more than a welfare mom bound to this couch forever? She looked at her child and wanted to believe Carol's words, that her child was more than the wrongs he'd committed, more than the life he had lived. Jeremy wanted to believe that his mother was more than the life she hadn't stirred herself to live. Silence filled the room.

In the corner of the living room were a few well-worn dusty

cardboard storage boxes long unopened throughout the many moves over the years, no black magic marker to identify their contents. Jeremy recognized them from the hall closet, competing for space with the vacuum cleaner and getting in the way when he hung his winter jacket. One had been opened; a flap stuck up like a tongue sticking out of a dead corpse. Textbooks, notebooks, yearbooks, photos, and scholastic awards from his mother's former life.

Jeremy walked over and pulled a textbook from the depths of the box. A math book that sparked the conversation. They spoke to each other as two adults for the first time. Not a lecture nor a scolding but a civil, substantive, and enlightening dialogue. Of math. Of school. Of grades. Of cheating. Of nicknames. Of Kelli. Of sex. Of children. Of father. Of Fire Island. Of college. Of prison. Of work. Of sickness. Of mac and cheese. Of apartment. Of farm. Of past. Of future. Of Saturday. Of Collins. Of Carol Morgan Spring. Of Roy. Of Sarah. Of her garden. Of bicycle. Of tractor. But not of plane, because that was his and his only, to share on his terms and his time. They talked late into the evening and shed light and some tears onto the mystery of their shared lives. Her son more than the wrongs he had committed, she more than the actions she hadn't taken. At conversation end she hugged her son, walked to the kitchen table, and ripped the progress report into three pieces.

CHAPTER 8

william henry gates III

IT LOOKED LIKE A comic book in color and stroke, the world rendered in shades from blue to magenta. Cities defined by their yellow glow at night, railroads thin black hashed lines, the color brown not for dirt but elevation. Modern-day aeronautical cartography no different than that of the Old World explorers, the Atlantic Ocean a marine blue but void of drawings of chimerical monsters.

"Dashed blue line?" Roy asked.

"Class D airspace," Jeremy answered confidently.

"Solid blue line?"

"Class B airspace."

"Good. Proper way to communicate to the air traffic controllers?"

"Three W's. Who we are. Where we are. What we want to do."

"Excellent. Airport with grass runways?"

"Empty circle?"

"Those are the best. You might even get a meal." Roy pointed to an airport as he looked over to the garden. "Right or left traffic pattern?"

"Right."

"Airport elevation?"

"Two hundred and eighty-five feet."

"Runway length?"

"One thousand three hundred feet." The sky was clear but Jeremy knew not to ask why they weren't going to fly. Roy's voice was heavy, the strain of her affliction etched in his face.

"Roy," Jeremy said.

"Yeah?"

"I just know she'll be better for Saturday."

"And how do you know that?"

"I just know," Jeremy said, his youthful enthusiasm contagious if only for a moment and drawing a fleeting grin from the old man.

"I'm looking forward to it. I am."

"Where's the best place you've ever flown?"

"Besides here?"

"Yeah."

"Just one?"

"Yeah."

Roy thought about it for a good minute. "It's more than one. It's the whole. Nothing stands on its own. All is connected, united. And it's when we forget that when we lose our way. But we always seem to find our way back, thank God—that's the greatness of this country. To me there's only one way to experience this country, and that's in an open-air cockpit flying from town to town. There is something true about landing on a man or woman's property. It's like being invited for dinner without the invite, none needed. Places like that still exist in this country. You can meet some of the best people you'll ever know. Sarah and I once flew all over the country for five weeks. That was our honeymoon, and it was the best experience of our young lives. The kindness and generosity of common folk opening their homes back then still exists. I know it does. I'm too old now, but I truly believe that you could take that plane today and experience what we did sixty years ago. We just circled a place on the chart and went.

Before you know it you'll get that opportunity one day and you'll be ready for it, I promise."

A well-read man, Roy understood the complexity of rules and regulations that were now part of flying, that his farm was a throwback to a simpler time. Roy didn't need to be told that technology made everything easier and more convenient; he lived in that world too. But he also knew that the skills he had learned as a young man, whether it was the proper way to fell a tree or fly an airplane, were timeless skills irrelevant of new technologies. Skills he was now teaching Jeremy.

He grudgingly understood that computers making decisions based on binary code would eventually supplant human judgment, and pilots would go the way of the dinosaur. But that day had not arrived, at least not yet, nor did he want to live to see it. That was why he ended each lesson not with math, physics, aerodynamics, nor meteorology.

"Son, you're not as good as you think. An airplane will kill you quicker than it will humble you. Flying is more than decision-making. It's about judgment, and judgment is about humility, and humility is about knowing what you don't know. Show me a computer with humility and I'll hand in my pilot wings. I had very little at your age, and you don't either. I know you've had a tough go at it. I can't imagine growing up without my father. He taught me many things and so did this farm. I also know the world has spit on you, and sometimes you got to spit back—you just gotta know when. You've made mistakes, everyone has, in life and in the plane. The lesson is to learn from them. You have. You've got good hands and a good head, but don't ever forget what you don't know. Even when you show a healthy respect for the skill and make the correct decisions, it still might not be enough. There are no guarantees in the plane or in life. Sometimes good isn't enough, sometimes you got to be lucky, sometimes the aviation gods are just against ya. You asked me once why I fly and I didn't have an answer. Well, I've been thinking about it since you asked. Everyone wants to be free. Free of the misery, free of the pain, free of the struggle, as free as in dream. But when you're up there, above it all looking down, you realize that you've become more connected with the world you're trying to free yourself from. The view is magnificent, the perspective even better. Dreams, books, or movies will have to do for others. For people like you and me, that's just not enough. That said, if I ever see that Billy Gates guy, I'll tell him I'll take carbon over silicon every time."

Jeremy pedaled away from the farm with a big smile. Since childhood he'd been categorized and marginalized by his school, his peers, society, his grandparents, his mom, and even himself. He never thought a conversation with an adult that started with "You're not as good as you think" and ending with "people like you" would be the most complimentary and uplifting words ever spoken to him.

CHAPTER 9

solo flight

THIRTY EARS OF LONG ISLAND sweet corn steamed on the large open grill, the smell of husk and butter filling the air. Children ran around the expanse of the farm's open field as if it were a prison break, and to the laughter and joy of the adults. Betty turned the corn on one grill, Gus the hot dogs, hamburgers, and flank steak marinated in honey, garlic, Worcestershire, and soy sauce on the other. The fragrance was heavenly.

The youngest was nine months, the oldest ninety—four generation of Americans sharing in the day. In attendance were great-grandparents, grandparents, sons, daughters, cousins, aunts, uncles, and a few who'd have a difficult time explaining their relationship but knew they were family somehow, every one of them a kid in some way. All celebrating family, a bind that links each generation to the ones who came before and those who follow.

Hand in hand with his beloved Sarah, Roy walked among the gathered spread out on blankets, beach chairs, and long picnic tables. Like newlyweds, the worries of the world gone if only for the day, their spirits lifted with every child's joyful scream and every parent's laugh.

Jeremy's job on this day was hayrides. He drove the tractor trailing a wagon lined with hay and gave tours of the farm. The children sang school songs as their tiny feet dangled from the side of the wagon. Swept up in the smell of food and the sound of song and laughter, Jeremy enjoyed the rides as much as his passengers. He wondered as he drove the tractor whether his mother had seen the note written on the back side of the progress report and left on the kitchen table. How could she not have?

Roy waved Jeremy over, signaling that the hayride express could continue after the midday meal. Kelli arrived with Carol and three other pregnant teenagers as lunch was being served, their appearance attracting interested looks from the adults. Roy welcomed Kelli, Carol, and her guests as Sarah walked over to each pregnant teenager, greeting them with a gentle hug and softly touching their bellies.

"Time to eat!" Roy announced. There would be no sermon, no reference to scripture, nor Gus speaking in Latin. God's benevolence was reflected in the people gathered, God's grace manifest on the land they walked.

Jeremy and Kelli sat side by side, their knees touching beneath the picnic table. In this imperfect world are perfect days to cherish and live in the moment and not to be saddened despite knowing that it will never be like this again. Nothing lasts forever except the earth and sky.

Kindred spirits met over potato salad and hot dogs. Betty talked of her Corvette, Carol of her Benz. Both agreed to disagree about the better car, but both agreed that green was best left as a color of a garden and not a vehicle. They spoke of men, the few they'd loved, the few more they'd married, and the many they'd outlived. Mothers talked of children, fathers of work, grandparents of death, and kids of video games.

Bellies full and conversation rich, lunch gave way to watermelon. Roy told Jeremy to pull the Cub from the barn. They climbed into the plane, Gus turned the prop, and the aircraft came alive. A mix of fear, joy, and interest spread among the kids as they held close to their parents. Their faces sticky with watermelon juice and seed they watched, captivated by the loud, yellow flying machine taxiing to the far end of the field.

Roy, a man of few words, said only one: "Three." Jeremy understood that Roy would not instruct. He would watch as the kids watched, as the parents watched, as Jeremy wished his mother would if she were there. *Not today, not now, there's too much to be grateful for.* He had to show more than a working knowledge and more than just a level of competence without prompt or input. He had to trust Roy's training and himself. Jeremy pushed the throttle forward and the fresh breeze cooled the cockpit. The Cub's tail lifted, the wing took flight, and Jeremy and Roy looked down as the crowd waved with watermelon rinds in hand. Jeremy was at ease in the air, the hard work of learning to fly now more than an expression of his will, but a learned skill that no one could take away. Roy was silent as Jeremy flew the pattern with skill and proficiency. There was no wasted movement of throttle, yoke, or pedals. He was at one with the plane, one with the world of flight, and one with the life he had created. Each landing was better than the last, and Roy's only words after the third landing were to taxi back to the barn. The Cub at idle, Roy exited the airplane, turned toward Jeremy, and looked him in the eyes. He pressed his thumb against Jeremy's heart, extended three fingers, saluted, and walked to the farmhouse thinking of the first time they'd met, how this wild-looking kid who smelled of skunk weed and fungus had walked into his life. *Life is the damnedest of things,* he mused, and chuckled at the thought. He had Jeremy to thank for reminding him that even though the grime of life eventually sticks and you can't wash it away, joy and hope were always possible.

Jeremy taxied to the far end of the farm, his senses heightened by being alone and the hundred eyes that gazed upon him. Alone but not lonely, a child of solitude, he'd always had the ability to entertain himself.

He pushed the throttles forward. The only judge now was gravity, not the gathered crowd, not an adult behind a desk wearing a black robe or a PhD in child psychology telling him that he was dumb. The Cub's tail lifted, Jeremy pulled back on the yoke, and the farm passed beneath the wing. The sound of the engine was more pronounced, the controls more responsive, and the Cub climbed quicker than he expected. It was without the weight and wisdom of Roy's presence. Solo flight, his and his alone. Jeremy's anxiety rose. His grip upon the controls tightened and his mind raced. It was quickly tempered by his training; Roy's voice as clear as the day he first heard it in his headphones resonated in his thoughts. Flying over the field Jeremy saw the crowd, necks craned, all looking skyward. Kelli sat on the tractor, its red paint matching her hair.

He banked the plane, aligning it with the grass runway, confident in the gift of this learned skill, hard-earned and gratefully received. There can be only one first solo flight, and Jeremy was trying to take it all in. It was dreamlike, but this was no dream. He flared and leveled the wing, turned his head toward the side window, the view forward blocked by the Cub's nose. The air beneath the wing and ground squeezed, then gently gave way as the Cub settled softly onto the grass. He would bookmark this moment in the deep recesses of his mind as it passed into memory, knowing that he'd probably forget the details but never its significance.

At the edge of his field of view he saw her standing among the cheering crowd, next to Carol as the Cub came to a stop. Clare's expression with her hands pressed against her face was as if to catch the mix of fear and bewilderment falling from it. Jeremy turned the Cub and taxied toward the far end of the field. Passing his adoring fan base—*This is how Lindbergh must have felt*—he gave his mom a wink and a wave. Carol lifted her wineglass skyward and joyously yelled "*Jer-e-me!*" The crowd followed her lead and repeated his name with childlike enthusiasm.

Clare stood there befuddled. How can this be? Who are these people? What is my son doing? There was a girl with a shock of red hair and distended belly standing on a tractor and cheering wildly with hands in the air. *That must be her!* she thought. She saw the bicycle that Jeremy had promised to return leaning against the barn and thought that this must be the place where he had found it. What is this place? She watched in amazement as an old black man in a wheelchair, his legs thin and fragile, willed himself to his feet and cheered mightily. She watched as a man signed the holy cross in the air, sprinkled water from his drink, and said Jeremy's name in prayer. And when a pregnant girl next to Carol said she wished he was her girlfriend, she asked herself, *How can this be?* Carol touched her arm and yelled, "Isn't this magnificent!"

A mother knows her son—how could she not? The airplane accelerated again, and the tail lifted. Clare now saw that Jeremy was more than the life he had lived. She now knew that he was more than the life she wished for him. Her emotions told her to run and she did, toward the small yellow plane, her emotions a mix of fear and joy. The Cub climbed skyward, and she stopped midfield and watched.

"My son, my son, my son, my son, my son!" she screamed, hopping in place like a child doing calisthenics. The crowd's attention now divided between the two.

Roy walked up to Clare. "This isn't a good place to stand," he said matter-of-factly.

"You, you're the one who left the note?" Clare said, her attention divided between the plane and Roy. "Is that your bicycle? Are you the one who ran him over with that tractor? How is he able to—my son! Oh my God, is he going to hurt himself! Is, is, is this even legal?!"

"Nope," Roy said laughing. "I can explain everything. But over there."

"I'm scared for my son!"

"If you don't move I'll be scared for you," Roy said. He offered her his hand as she looked at the yellow plane's approach. Roy led her away from the center of the field like a reluctant child. A few feet from the runway's edge he turned her around. Jeremy flared and the Cub slowed and settled before them, the displaced air gently washing over Roy and Clare, her body awash with the visceral touch of flight as the Cub came to a stop. She was speechless. Taxiing back for his last takeoff and landing of the day, he passed Clare and Roy. Tears streamed from her eyes. Jeremy waved and she read his lips: "I love you too."

Most children eventually see through the clutter of their parents' lives, as they do their own, and Jeremy knew his mom's goodness and love absolute. And that love and faith were the foundation on which both could become. This day was equally hers as his.

Clare clutched Roy, warmed by his touch as they walked back to the farmhouse. She leaned on him, not knowing if it was her weight or his age that caused the slow but determined gait in his walk. It didn't matter. There was a lyrical quality about his every movement, every stride, and every step. He led her with meaning and purpose, and it calmed her to realize that he knew the ground he walked on and the world he lived in like no one she'd ever met.

Dixon stayed on his feet for Jeremy's third and final landing, his legs finally giving out after Jeremy taxied next to the barn, shut off the engine, and exited the Cub. Dixon saluted him and the young man returned the gesture before walking over to shake Dixon's hand.

"Congratulations kid," said Dixon. I'd get up—"

"Mr. Dixon, you've been standing for eighty-five years," Jeremy said. "Thank you."

"No son, thank you. We've needed new blood around here, and you were just the ticket."

As Jeremy starting walking toward his mom, Dixon called after him. "Moms can wait, girlfriends can't! If I had your legs I'd go kiss the girl!"

Jeremy looked at Kelli standing atop the tractor and then his mom standing next to Roy. What to do?

"Kiss the girl! Kiss the girl!" Carol yelled. Again the gathered group followed her lead and repeated the chant. Jeremy ran toward the tractor, climbed up, and stood nose to nose with his girl.

"That was amazing, Jeremy," Kelli said.

"Thanks," Jeremy said with a big smile.

"Are you embarrassed as I am?"

"Nope. Why would I be embarrassed?"

"I'm kind of shy. I've never kissed—"

"Kissed a pilot before?"

"I was going to say in front of an audience."

"There's always a first time for everything."

"I guess. Just a cute kiss, okay?"

"S-u-r-e," Jeremy said. He cupped her face in his hands and brought her toward him. Their lips touched, then she exhaled in willful surrender as he kissed her as she'd never been kissed before, to the roar of the crowd.

"Damn, I wish I were young again!" Betty yelled. "To the newest member of the One of Us club!"

CHAPTER 10

death

THE YOUNG LADIES at the front desk at the South Shore Assisted Living Home had the long look of sadness as Roy entered with coffee in hand. He said his polite hellos, their response muted, signed in, and started walking toward Sarah's room. He had long stopped watching the news, but on this day the television caught his eye.

"The task is considered to be one of the most challenging for a human pilot. The unmanned drone, the size of a fighter jet, landed on the USS *George H. W. Bush* off the coast of Virginia. The procedure was performed exclusively by the drone's built-in computer . . ."

Roy stood there for a moment not knowing what to think. Surprise was the first emotion that presented itself. He didn't think he'd see this in his lifetime. Obsolescence and a bit of anger trailed close behind and were then punctuated with a small laugh. *Christ, I'm pushing a century,* he thought. *What did I expect? Shit, perhaps it's a good thing; it will save a few aviators' lives, but what about the poetry of flying?* Then his thoughts turned to Sarah as he walked to her room.

Dr. R., a nurse, and an attendant stood beside Sarah's bed. Roy had understood that this day would arrive, but he hadn't expected that today would be the day. "She refuses to eat," the doctor had said. Roy knew this was the last stage before death. He'd thought the memories of Saturday would carry her for at least a few more months, but perhaps she wanted to pass before the memory of it was lost. He handed his coffee to the attendant, politely asked for everyone to leave, and sat next to her. He smoothed her hair and stroked her arm. She was unusually cold, her breathing labored and irregular. He kissed her on her button nose, her rigid muscles relaxed, and her long, dull stare softened. He softly promised to make the buttermilk pancakes himself if she'd just eat. Please eat.

With a wet cloth he moistened her dry lips, their curves as beautiful as the first day he'd laid eyes on her, and applied lip balm. He retold the story of the day they'd met in civics class and then his favorite, when they fell in love in the garden of Eve. Nothing. She'd always responded in some way. Nothing.

He couldn't live without her, but he knew she couldn't live this way. They agreed a long time ago: no feeding tube, no breathing tube, diapers the last indignity. And home. Of course home for the last breath, her last living wish. She was coming home.

The living room of the farmhouse became Sarah's bedroom, her rented hospital bed too large and her medical needs too great to be attended in their small bedroom. But Betty made sure that the comfort of Sarah's bedroom filled the space. She discarded the hospital bed sheets and pillows for Sarah's own. Before Sarah arrived, Betty had washed and line-dried her bedding, quilt, and comforter, and when Sarah was tucked into the bed for the first time and looked to see her nightstand and lamp beside the bed, she drew the sheets to her nose, drew a deep breath, and smiled, warmed by the smell of sunshine and the farm.

The Hollywood ending Roy had imagined as he held her hand in the back of the ambulance on their return to the farm quickly vanished as Roy soon realized Sarah's comfort required far more than his will and good intentions. At the nursing home it required a staff of people, and it would take the same at home. His family of friends were there every day. The needs of maintaining the farmhouse hadn't waned with Sarah's sickness, and over the years much had gone by the wayside. A private man, Roy was embarrassed by its decline and felt exposed and raw having so many people in the house. But he was also thankful. He was grateful for his extended family, all those years of helping others and now them helping him.

It was more than routine housekeeping and shopping, more than laundry and cooking, more than the women helping Roy bath, dress, and turn her in the bed when she groaned in discomfort. The One of Us club watched him as closely as they did Sarah. And on those days when he felt that he was going to drown in sorrow and his eyes turned hateful, he took comfort in knowing that he could leave Sarah in the loving hands of his friends. At first, he never left her side, his greatest fear her dying without him there. But as the good doctor said on his first visit to the farmhouse, death is always difficult to predict, yet modern medicine was a far second to love—"You will know," he promised. Roy slowly warmed to the doctor's opinion and every day walked the perimeter of the farm to feel the life of the grass and earth beneath him and hear the wind make the trees sing. He drew fresh air into his lungs and cleared his head and always returned better than when he left. Sarah was his religion, the soil his cathedral, but forever doesn't apply to humans, only to the earth and sky.

It was an unusual sight, Clare sitting on the bicycle rack, holding tight as Jeremy pedaled to the farm to drop her off before heading to school. The other mothers on the block, pajama clad, watched Jeremy and Clare ride by as they dragged their empty garbage cans to the curb, their kids safely on the school bus.

Every day Clare, like clockwork, arrived early and stayed late, Jeremy returning to the farm after school with Kelli to help out in any way possible. Carol came in the evenings with a home-cooked meal prepared by her chef that she took complete credit for. They ate on the deck just a few feet from the living room, in the lumens of starlight and candlelight, the sounds of crickets chirping and birds cooing as comforting as the meal itself.

The word *family* bounced around in Jeremy's brain with three generations of women in front of him. Outsiders might call them the old, the forgotten, the discarded, and the yet-to-be-born bastard. To Jeremy they were family, his family. Grandmother, mother, and girlfriend. He was born lost and remained lost until finding this place and these people, yet all around him was the dark shadow of death. Despite this he was more hopeful than ever. He understood that Sarah would pass but Roy had the farm, his friends of fifty years, and his friendship. *He'll miss her but we'll be here for him. That will be enough.*

Love of a woman, the fruits of which Jeremy was just becoming familiar, was as sweet as anything he'd experienced. But great literature, poetry, and music grew best in mixed soil. And who to share in this great feast but the one you love most? What happens when they are gone? What is a young man to think who's never experienced the anguish of a newly empty bed? Of breakfast suddenly eaten alone? Of going through the day never again getting to hear her laugh? Or of looking out at her untended garden?

Sometimes life itself gives way before the body does, and then what do you do? Roy took solace in the evening meal more for the company than for the food. He had eaten less and less as Sarah's health declined, and when she stopped eating altogether, he stopped as well. He had no hunger for life but enjoyed the spirited conversations among the ladies. He sat there knowing what his Sarah would say and would smile at the thought. When Kelli took notice, she prepared him a plate and set it in front of him. He frowned at her as the others looked on. But Red would have none of it. She leaned in and whispered in his ear. His eyes welled and his skin flushed. It took a few minutes, but slowly he began to eat for the first time in days.

By meal's end Clare was calling Kelli "Red." Carol called Clare by her full name, "Clare Darcy McNeal" and Kelli called both Carol and Clare "Mom." Jeremy didn't know what to make of it, but as Roy explained, men aren't supposed to. Roy returned to Sarah's side, stroked her hair, and whispered the name they'd given their son in their youthful days of their young life which now would live again.

◆ ◆ ◆

Scripture said, "Six days you shall labor, but on the seventh day you shall rest; even during the plowing season and harvest you must rest." The good doctor was correct, and on the evening of the seventh night Roy asked Gus to give the sacrament of the last rites. Gus leaned over the bed, his rosaries in one hand and holy water in the other. He gave the Eucharist in Latin and the last sentence in English. Roy had never been more moved by the spirituality of his dear friend.

"May the Lord Jesus Christ protect you and lead you to eternal life," Gus said. "Amen."

"Amen," Roy said.

"She will not die alone; the Lord will be with her."

"I know. That last line. Could you?"

"Roy—"

"Every time I fly you pray."

"That's because flying is a new invention."

"My lord, Gus!"

"Don't take the Lord's name in vain."

"Just pretend I'm going flying. Just this once. Please, Gus."

"Don't you understand! The boy needs you. Your friends need you. We all love you! All of us can help you get through this. We can have more Wednesdays, Roy. More Saturdays!"

"You don't just get through this!"

"People do every day!"

"You love God? Well, do ya?!"

"Of course, more than—"

"Life! And that's my point. This woman is my life! Just this once," Roy said.

"I . . . don't understand. Your life is a gift. How could you?" With tears in his eyes Gus looked at Roy and then looked toward the floor. "May the Lord Jesus protect you and Sarah and lead you . . . both . . . together into eternal life."

"Thank you, Gus," Roy said. "Thank you, my friend."

Sarah had lost the ability to speak, even the groans fell silent, yet the pain was still evident in her eyes. He knew it was time, her body falling into itself like the cornstalks after harvest. That evening, the twitch in her fingers awoke him. He stood beside her bed, his hand in hers, thinking she would say good-bye. Roy wanted to believe she tried to summon the last scrap of life within her to say something, to focus her eyes on him, to feel his touch, his presence, his smell. Nothing. It ended with the rattle of her last breath and her jaw went slack.

He stood there in shock, his compass, his companion, his life, lover, friend, and wife now gone. She was now memory, a lifetime of remembrances now in his solitary possession. He held onto her hand well into the night and repeated his undying love in story and song. The long shadows of the morning sun broke through the tall pines, casting fingers of everlasting light onto the farm. Jeremy and Clare rode up, Clare sensing something different this morning. She sent Jeremy on his way, the wisdom of which she would always be thankful for. What use in a child seeing not only the dead, but the suffering of the living? He'd have his share in this life, but not today. But Jeremy was having none of it. He raced toward school to pick up Kelli and return as fast as he could pedal.

Clare walked to Roy and gently separated his hand from Sarah's. He didn't resist, perhaps out of exhaustion, or just plain shock. She walked him out onto the porch and sat him at the picnic table. The morning sun seemed to warm him, his shoulders relaxed, but his vacant stare would not focus. The others arrived, familiar with the smell of death, and sat in silence. Betty made the phone call, and before the doctor arrived each entered the living room to pay their last respects, Gus anointing the holy oil upon her forehead.

A declaration of death was signed by the doctor and sealed not by the state, but the sound of the zipper closing the length of the body bag. Roy groaned, stood, and hurriedly walked away from the farmhouse as the two men from the funeral home gathered her body. He would not look, could not look as the hearse pulled away.

He walked to the middle of the field, his back facing the farmhouse. He suddenly couldn't picture any of those times when, his work done and returning home, the smell of her cooking and her warm, welcoming smile were there for him.

Jeremy and Kelli rode up to see everyone gathered on the porch looking out at Roy standing alone in the middle of the field. The club looked fragile, weathered, and worried. This death felt different, as if it might tear them all asunder. Roy stood alone in the open field, but to Kelli it was no different than her nights alone in the darkened public stalls thinking thoughts of death and wondering whether she had the will to live or the hope of anyone saving her. She grabbed Jeremy's hand and led him toward Roy.

Roy felt her thumb gently pressing into his palm and then her hand wrapping around his. A touch, an expression of the physical world. A life preserver sent to help the drowning. It brought Roy back to the present, a warm pulse of the girl in one hand, the boy now in the other, both guides back to the living.

The others looked on from the porch as he turned toward them, gathered himself, and slowly walked back with the children in tow. "Let us eat," he said. He had no appetite but it was a kind gesture, an attempt at normalcy to comfort those around him. Roy wanted all of them to know that life must and will go on— at least for them.

The women prepared a simple meal of roast beef and turkey sandwiches with soda and chips. They ate in silence, the midday chirp of crickets and birds comforting their anguish and pushing back against death's silence.

"Cliff, still alive down there?" Roy asked Cliff, who was sitting at the far end of the table.

"I think so," Cliff said.

"Fifty years never heard you this quiet," Roy said.

For as long as anyone could remember, Cliff had always had a response. But not now.

"I know, death will do that," Roy said. "You do realize that Deacon Gus will lead your funeral mass."

"Not if I outlive him," Cliff said to the laugh of the crowd, and even Roy broke a smile.

All of us will stare down death and lose, so why not laugh as the Buddha laughs? It doesn't disrespect the dead but honors them. It was okay, and for a brief moment they all thought Roy would get through these uncharted waters without his beloved. Roy thanked his friends for all they had done, and when the midday meal was over, all that stood between Roy and being alone for the first time in sixty-five years was Jeremy, who refused to leave, convinced the old man would be all right as long as he was there.

"Go home, son," Roy said. "It's okay. I'll be fine."

"Will you?" Jeremy asked.

"I will. Go home."

"I am home."

"Come on, I got something to give ya."

They walked to the barn and there, resting on the tail of the Cub, was Roy's brown leather Navy flight jacket.

"I was going to give it to ya after you soloed, but—" Roy said.

"I can't take it," Jeremy said.

"It's a gift."

"It's a parting gift! If I don't take it you can't go!" Jeremy said, his voice trembling.

"No life goes according to script, especially the one we hope for as a child. This is for you. A thank you. I've had a great life, an extraordinary life, and luck has been with me, the list too long to say. It's a great world and don't let anyone tell you different."

"Don't, Roy! You can't leave! My fa—"

"Son. I promise I'll be here as long as I can."

"I don't believe you!"

"Come on now. I've always kept my word, haven't I?"

"You . . . have," Jeremy said, unconvinced.

"Go 'head, put it on." Roy took the jacket from the Cub's tail and held it open as Jeremy slipped in his right arm, then his left, as Roy pushed it over his shoulders. Jeremy ran his hand over the sleeves, the jacket warm and comforting as a hug. The fabric cuffs were frayed and the zipper rusted, but the well-worn jacket and all it stood for moved Jeremy.

"I know, real smooth," Roy said. "Damn leather aged better than me. Goat skin, not that cow leather crap and pleather they issue now."

The jacket had a distinct animal smell, not of mold or age but of the textured scent of sacrifice. The smell captured Jeremy's imagination. He could see Roy with leather skullcap and jacket, strapped into his TBM Avenger, flying over the vast Pacific defending country, home, and family.

"Lamb's wool in the inside," Roy said.

Jeremy opened the jacket. Sewn into the inside were two flags.

On one side a large American flag. On the other, Chinese calligraphy below the flag of a nation he didn't recognize.

"My God, I'd forgotten how beautiful she was. Those legs, that waist, her smile," Roy said. On the back of the jacket, the artwork skillfully drawn and painted by a fellow squadron mate, a scantily clad Sarah lying seductively on the wing of his Avenger, her legs skyward, cleavage in full view, and her name in script stretching the length of the jacket's shoulders. She was Roy's pinup girl and his skin went flush thinking of her at eighteen. She'd been sick for so long his memories and even his dreams were of both of them aged.

"I wore this jacket only twice when I got back from the war," Roy said.

"I would have worn it every day," Jeremy said.

"I know. I would have too! Sarah was a bit embarrassed when she first saw it but boy, first time in town walking with my girl and this jacket, it turned heads. We walked into every store and she made sure everyone saw it. All those double takes from men and women alike and the biggest smile I'd ever seen on her face. Done a lot of walking in my life, but not as much as I did that day."

"So why'd you stop wearing it?"

"Three words: mother-in-law. Eve was a good woman, but when she saw this jacket she gave me a tongue lashing. She said only way to make amends was going to church and confessing."

"Confess what?"

"That's what I asked her. To ask God to forgive me for depicting her daughter in an ungodly, unseemly way."

"Well, did ya go?" Jeremy asked.

"Had to! No choice. She even went with me. But I had a plan. Gus was studying to be a deacon at Our Lady of the Snow Catholic Church. We spent an hour in the confessional playing cards and laughing our asses off."

Jeremy ran his hand across the USN lettering stamped on the inside leather flap and again on the outside across the frayed gold fabric of the wings stitched above the heart.

"Never much talked about the war. Sobering, all the death and destruction. I was five years older than you are now. Nineteen when I became a Navy pilot. It was a different time. Some things were better, some things worse. Now it's your time, Jeremy."

"Nineteen," Jeremy murmured. He had never pictured Roy as a young man, as if he'd been born aged, wise and with gray hair. But now he wore this jacket, the skin of Roy's younger life, and could picture the nineteen-year-old wearing it seventy years ago.

Barely legible below the frayed gold fabric of the navy wings was Roy's name in faded gold leaf. LT. ROY HIGGINS, USN. *What's in a name? Everything.* And for the first time since they'd met Jeremy knew Roy as a young man, Roy's zeal for life and determined grit at nineteen as well as ninety. He took off the jacket and looked at the artwork on the back.

"Wow, she's beautiful."

"Easy son, she's mine. You've got a good young lady. Wise beyond her years, and she's got a hold of you, son."

"I know."

"You'll both be fine. I can promise you that too."

"How can you be so sure, Roy?"

"Because this life will always provide. You may not under-stand it, but you have to trust yourself and the world will provide. I'm not a religious man but I believe in God. And like I told you, 'cause I see a lot of you in me. Our paths are not that different. You've fought to get where you are today. You knew there was something more to this world and you found it. You wouldn't go away and you wouldn't quit. A lesser man would have chosen an easier path. You got skin in the game now. I'm proud of you, kid. Now it's time to go home."

He pressed his thumb against Jeremy's chest as he did before he soloed. The wings of gold between heart and hand. And Jeremy understood. It takes heart, mind, and hand to live a purposeful life.

Roy walked toward the farmhouse as Jeremy climbed onto his bike.

"I'll be back tomorrow after school."

"Good. The grass needs cutting. And don't forget, the tractor needs two quarts of oil. Take care of the engine and it will always take care of you."

"Will do," Jeremy said as he pedaled away into the darkness.

"And kid!"

"Yeah?" Jeremy asked, barely able to hear his friend over the sound of the bicycle's tires spinning on the gravel as they lengthened the distance between them.

"Fuck comportment!"

CHAPTER 11

transcendence

ROY FELT THE FRESH sting of aftershave. He combed his hair and tried to give himself a trim, but saw that he was making a mess of things and quickly abandoned the effort. Sarah used to cut his hair. A shave and a comb would have to do. She'll understand, he told himself. He splashed on some Old Spice cologne, Sarah's favorite, and put on his best suit.

The long evening over, Roy sat relaxed in the deep seat of his favorite living room chair. A place of much living. Her seat next to his, the distance between the two less than a hand away. And on those nights when one was immersed in a novel and the other wanted attention, the touch of hand upon hand was all that was needed. He looked over at the empty hospital bed, the sheets and mattress gone. How many had died on that rent-a-bed, he wondered. *You should die in your own bed. No bed should have goddamn wheels! There for cars and tractors and airplanes, for God's sake!*

On the nightstand Sarah's glasses refracted the warm light of the bed lamp, and Roy remembered how they rested on the bridge of her beautiful nose. He could see his bespectacled wife look at him after the touch of his hand upon hers and hear her say, "Poetry, music, and literature are my food and drink, you and the farm, my love and life."

A warm calmness comforted him as the adrenaline began to fade. The bodily aches and pains returned as certain as the morning twilight appears behind the steel grey sky. The echo of the young man he once was was now gone. A last taste of youth. *The future is yours, Jeremy, and so is she. Take care of her. To the defiant, to the rebels, and to the journey. You'll be fine. I promise. I promise! I'm going to be with Sarah now.*

His wedding photograph, framed in oak shaped by his hands from the tree where they first kissed, lay in his lap. The trees whistled and the southerly wind carried the salted sea air through the open windows. Roy drew a deep breath, comforted by its familiar warmth as it carried him to memories of his youth. "We are all of the sea," he muttered as he fell into a gentle sleep and the hereafter.

In dream as in life his thoughts were always of her, but in this his last they were free of old age and illness, free of tragedy and heartbreak, and free of death. And like the Stearman standing on its tail, its outstretched wings wrapped in the magnificence of the blue sky, his life, their life, was transcendent.

Roy Higgins sits comfortably in the open rear cockpit of his new Boeing-Stearman and his newlywed wife sits in the front, her excitement bright as her golden hair dancing in the benevolent wind. Her perfume mixes with the exhaust of oil and spent gasoline and wafted over him. She is his compass, his companion, his life, lover, friend, and wife. The early morning sunrise paints colors on the Stearman's windscreen, the familiar rhythmic vibration of the Lycoming engine comforting as they head toward the horizon. With earth below and blue sky above they will spend this day as they will every day: together and forever young. At day's end, when the horizon sleeps and the veil of the moon shines its incandescent light upon the world, they will return to the farm and make love beneath the wing of the Stearman.

They were together again. As he had promised, as he had wished, as he had dreamed, as he had willed.

CHAPTER 12

rule 1-3: f*ck comportment

JEREMY BIKED TOWARD SCHOOL, not knowing that heaven was closed that day. The dark gray sky, the color of a steel plate, looked as if its weight would collapse and crush all who lived upon the earth. He arrived at school to see police cars outnumbering the short buses, cops more numerous than students. The gray sky obediently changed to the colors of the flashing lights atop the police cruisers. *Another fight. Not my problem.*

Jeremy locked up his bicycle and waited in line to enter the razor-wired school. When it was his turn the wand never beeped, but a police sergeant watching closely told him that everyone must be patted down. There was tension in the cold, damp air, but as each student knew, tension was built into Frontier. It was part of the curriculum. Students walked unfazed, smiling and giggling as two officers escorted each student to class, chains around ankles the only thing missing.

Police officers were gathered behind caution tape sealing off the nurse's office. They milled about the open doorway taking photos and scribbling notes onto notepads as they muttered to each other in low voices. Two police officers with the letters CSI on their uniforms were scrutinizing a can of white spray paint in a plastic bag labeled EVIDENCE.

As Jeremy passed the open doorway of the nurse's office he saw the linoleum floor littered with pills, thousands of them, as they slowly dissolved in the colorful stew of prescription liquids from the four gutted refrigerators against the far wall. One of the refrigerator doors swung freely and on the front of the stainless steel door scrawled in white paint were the letters 'ODD' inside a circle with three lines through it. Jeremy smiled at the poor artistry and wondered what it meant.

"Didn't steal a thing," Jeremy's escort said. "Trashed tens of thousands of dollars of prescription meds."

"Really."

"Yeah, you won't be getting your fix today. Prescription meds my ass. Bunch of addicts in here. Crock of shit. Give me five minutes with that kid and I'll straighten his punk ass out."

"You won't have any problems with me," Jeremy said. He was looking forward to seeing Kelli, showing her his jacket, completing course modules in math, science, and history, and then getting on the American Harvester and bush-hogging the expanse of the farm. That was his fix.

"Thank God my kids are home schooled," the police officer said. "Education is everything. Everything."

"It's the only way out of here," Jeremy said. They arrived at his trailer and the police officer knocked on the door.

"Level 4. All doors are locked. We see you unescorted out of the classroom and we'll lock your ass up. Though I don't know why that'd concern you. Jail seems like a step up from this place."

Collins opened the door and the stale light from the trailer reflected in his beady eyes.

"He's late."

"Not his fault," the police officer said. "Wands, pats, and double escorts today. We got backed up. Let him in. Unless you want him arrested."

"Don't tempt me," Collins said as he reluctantly stepped aside. His encounter with Carol was never far from his mind, and the memory unconsciously manifested itself in clenched hands every time he saw Jeremy.

Jeremy walked past Collins and to his desk. He hugged Kelli and showed her the jacket. Collins had the power to let it go, but the anguish of a failed life and the urgent desire for revenge would not let him. The pain that gnawed incessantly within him needed relief, and he did as the alchemist did and transformed it to a baser metal. And when he saw Jeremy hug Kelli it confirmed his suspicions. He hurried to his desk and picked up the Frontier Academy District Policies and Procedures Manual sitting next to the Life section of the *Times*. His eyes lit up brighter with every line he read. Dumb cops, he thought. How could they have missed it? He read the policy three times, the third time aloud, the pitch of his voice fluctuating with every word. The students looked up, startled by his fervor and the malice that rose with every word.

"Rule 1-3! Student dress code," he shouted. "Students are prohibited from wearing clothing that depicts profanity, vulgarity, obscenity, or violence! Clothing shall be free of inflammatory, suggestive, or other inappropriate writing, advertisement, or artwork! Ill-fitted garments are not acceptable! As are garments that are too small so as to reflect immodesty or too large so as to appear to be falling off the body!"

And the heavens closed. A scantily clad Sarah lying suggestively on the wing, the bombs beneath her phallic. To some it could be provocative, vulgar, or obscene. Not to the nineteen-year-old fighting in the South Pacific, trying stay alive and yearning to come home to his girl, the artwork on his jacket a reminder of life and love and the only counter to death and violence.

Mr. Collins stood up and pointed at Jeremy. "That jacket is mine!"

he said. Jeremy looked back in bewilderment. "Off with it!"

"But—"

"But nothing!"

"I'll go home before you—"

"No you won't!"

Jeremy looked at Kelli, the dark gray sky the color of a steel plate about to crush him. "That little shit ain't taking my jacket," he said.

"Please give him the jacket," Kelli said. "I'll make sure Carol gets it back."

"We'll see about that!" Mr. Collins said. He walked around his desk and toward Jeremy. "Earn your pay, square badge!" Collins shouted. The plump armed guard, unoffended by the insult, stood and approached Jeremy from behind as Collins advanced from the front.

"Off with it!" Collins said.

Jeremy looked at Kelli and extended his arms outward. The shadow on the floor: to some Jesus on the cross, to others just another teenage perp getting what he deserved, to Jeremy the Stearman standing on its tail against the vast backdrop of the sky.

"You don't want to do this," the guard said.

"Neither do you," Jeremy said.

The other students cackled and howled, no longer lethargic from the meds pumped daily into their bodies. "Hit the pricks!" one shouted.

"You're one mistake away from Albany," the guard said. "Just give him the jacket."

"Never!" Jeremy said. "This jacket stands for love not hate! Peace not war! And to the man who gave it to me, truth and goodness and the beauty of this life. It's everything you're not and everything I'm trying to become."

He looked at Kelli and saw her mind racing behind her nervous, watery eyes. Every kid at Frontier knew that incarceration was one bad decision away, and not always a bad decision of their making.

"Bravo, young convict. Bravo," Collins said. "Now give me that jacket!"

If only it were as simple as the wave of a magic wand. If only he'd been bitten by a radioactive spider as a young man, or discovered his wizard powers as a child. If only he had been born of a dying planet a galaxy away and sent here with superhuman powers. But for Jeremy there was only one choice. He felt the heavy hands of the guard grab him by the back of the neck.

"Fuck you!" Jeremy said. He tried to break free, shoving backward Collins, who crashed into a sea of seats as the other students howled in delight. The guard pushed Jeremy face-first against the wall, firmly pinning his head against it. The thump and the shudder that rippled through the trailer spurred the other students into an audible frenzy. There was a flash of light and a sharp pain concussed throughout Jeremy's skull, and for an instant he was back on the bus being beaten by Big Mac. With the ease of palming a basketball, the guard held Jeremy's skull with one hand as he horse-collared the jacket with the other. His arms now freed, Jeremy pushed against the wall, but it was of no use. The guard outweighed Jeremy by one hundred pounds and used his leverage like a skilled wrestler.

After untangling himself from the spilled chairs, Collins rushed forward and grabbed the collar and pulled. Jeremy heard the tear before he felt it, the aged stitching giving way, and screamed as if it were his own skin. Thought and reason left him and he shook with anger. He flailed, trying to free himself with no success.
"If your mom would have listened!" Collins shouted as he yanked a second time. Jeremy threw an elbow that landed on the security guard's chin, drawing blood.

"That's assault!" Collins shouted. "You're going upstate!"

Unfazed, the guard pressed Jeremy's forehead against the wall.

Jeremy's brain expanded with rage. His thoughts left him, he was an animal. He threw his legs back hoping to catch any body part; again, nothing. Collins grabbed the front of the jacket, trying to pull it over Jeremy's shoulders, only to rip off the jacket's nametag. ROY HIGGINS, LT.USN in letters of gold leaf fell to the linoleum floor.

"I know what's best!" Collins shouted. "If your mother listened! If you listened!"

And how 'bout that other fantasy? The one that said that Jeremy's righteousness would win out because the truth was on his side. Better take the vampires and the green puppet bullshit, because in this trailer of higher learning Collins was judge, jury, and executioner. How dare you challenge City Hall! You'll be scorned, condemned, convicted, and incarcerated. Rage against nothing! Medicate your children! Medicate your children!

"Stop it! Stop it!" Kelli screamed.

The jacket now torn beyond repair and Jeremy exhausted of body and spirit, Collins yanked it free. *You've fought to get where you are today / You wouldn't go away / You wouldn't quit / A lesser man would have chosen an easier path.* Roy's words resonated in Jeremy as tears filled his eyes, his anger now resignation.

"What good can come from this?" Jeremy mumbled to himself.

"Let him go!" Kelli said. The guard looked at Collins and awaited instruction.

"Not until I get a police officer in here," Collins said. "That's the good that will come of this!"

"No!" Kelli shouted as she ran to the door and blocked it. "No!"

"Young lady, pregnant or not I'll walk right through you!" Collins said.

But then the other students began to stand. "No you won't," one said as the group stood in front of the door with Kelli.

"You'll all go upstate!" Collins thundered. "Every one of you!"

"Not today," said one.

"Not today, *mijo*," said another.

The wind carries you to places wanted and unwanted. *You got legs, use them. You can't fly this plane without the rudder. Feet! Young man. Feet. Gotta lean into it. Redirect the ship! The physics of flight and fight*, Roy's voice as clear as the first time they had flown together. His head still pinned to the wall, Jeremy picked up both of his legs from the floor, firmly planted them against the wall, and pushed, finally breaking free of the guard's firm grip. They fell backward and the guard's head struck a bolted desk, knocking him out cold.

"Out of the way!" Collins shouted. But the students had the numbers and Collins knew it. "Fools, all of you! All of you will end upstate! Is that what you want?!" The kids stood firm. Collins ran toward his desk and reached for the phone. He had started to dial when Jeremy grabbed the base of the phone and threw it against the wall.

"If I'm going upstate I'm going to earn it, you piece of shit!" Jeremy said. His eyes a rage, his mind animal he lunged forward and shoved Collins violently against the wall, and the trailer shuddered again as Collins fell to the floor.

"*No!*" Kelli said. She ran from the door and forced herself between Jeremy and a dazed Collins slumped in the corner of the trailer.

"Get out of the way!" Jeremy said.

"No, Jeremy! No!"

"There's nothing left! I'm done. I'm going away. I never had a chance."

"Then you'll have to go through me!" Kelli grabbed Jeremy's face and drew him close. She stared into his eyes, trying to exorcise the demonic possession of animal rage, a rage he thought he had abandoned when he found her, Roy, and a world filled with wonder and knowledge.

Her touch, her eyes, her love, her sheer will was a reminder, a beacon from the world he'd fought to create. *The gods can't stand the happiness of mortals, but she has been there for me, always there for me.* All was not lost, he was hers, and no one could take that away.

"You'll all be charged with kidnapping," Collins said as he lifted himself from the floor. "All of you, and that's real time in federal prison! What are you going to do now, convict? Half the Suffolk County Police Department is outside! You think they're going to believe you? Any of you? You don't have a chance." Collins cautiously walked to his desk and looked at the kids barricading the doorway. "This is between him and me! It has nothing to do with any of you! Let me out and all will be forgotten."

They were children, every one of them, hard-knock kids who'd drawn life's short straw. All you had to do was look past their tough exteriors and see the evident fright in their eyes.

"*No!*" Kelli said. "Stay where you are!"

"I got all day!" Collins said. He sat back down at his desk and picked up the Times, searching for the next section to read as if it were just another school day. It was then that she saw it. It was then that she knew. The daily attendance sheet sitting underneath the newspaper. A way out, she thought. Every day it was her job to deliver it to the principal's office. Once there he could easily exit the school unnoticed. She handed it to Jeremy.

"Walk. Don't run," she said.

"I'm done running!" he said.

"You've done nothing wrong."

"They won't believe us! He's right."

"They'll have to. I'll make them. The truth matters!" Kelli said.

"It's his truth, their truth, not ours!"

"No! You wouldn't have gone to Fire Island, you wouldn't have learned to fly, you wouldn't have found Roy, and you wouldn't have cared to know me as anything more than a teenage pregnant slut. It does matter!"

He had long stopped underestimating her. This redheaded lioness refused to abandon hope, her own, his, theirs, and the world's. He'd given her his heart. He couldn't say no.

"Okay," he said.

"You've got five minutes," she said. She turned to the students blocking the door. "Give him five minutes. Please."

"And if they—" Jeremy said.

"Then I will find you."

With the sleeve of her blouse she wiped the sweat from his face. She combed his disheveled hair with her fingers. She pulled him closer and her determined look and her trusting touch moved him to believe that all would be well. Today she led, Saturday he led. Was that not love? Was that not marriage?

"They'll find you!" Collins yelled from his desk. "Prison is your future!"

"Go," Kelli said. "We'll figure this out."

Jeremy took a last look at Collins.

"No! Me," said Kelli. "I'll find you!" He looked at her and exited the classroom.

Jeremy walked through the school courtyard, the late morning overcast now, a light rain, his every step reddening his vision with pain. He walked briskly, wanting to run but knowing not to. To each passing police officer he brandished his talisman and in a firm voice said, "I'm taking the attendance sheet for Mr. Collins's class to the principal's office." None stopped him as he made his way into the rear entrance of the administrative building and past a group of police officers.

Standing inside the school's main entrance the principal listened intently as the lead detective described the contents of the video surveillance. Shaken by the events of the day, the principal stood transfixed in disbelief as the detective described the culprit. Jeremy saw his opportunity, walked up, and handed him the attendance sheet, the principal giving him a cursory look, neither cop nor principal interested as he walked out the front door.

Jeremy walked past the bicycle rack, past his Schwinn Autocycle Super Deluxe as he left it chained to the metal bars, bars that reminded him of his cell in juvenile detention. But his key to the bicycle lock was in the shredded leather pocket of his jacket. He walked away from the school, and after passing the last cop car he sprinted toward the farm. It was back to foot speed, bike speed no longer an option.

The wheel is come full circle. Shakespeare.

In a full sprint, he never once looked back nor slowed down. His lungs screamed for him to stop and his heart felt as if it was trying to burst from his chest. His skull ablaze and neck raw, the cutting rain glass shards against his skin, Jeremy kept on running.

Jeremy scanned the horizon, his gaze and thoughts fixed on the place he called home. *There's no horizon in jail.* His legs and heart were fueled by a hope he couldn't define. All he saw was her. His lungs were heated, his clothes were drenched with a mix of sweat and rain, the gray overcast had a jailhouse florescence, and the rainfall had the smell of bleach and Pine-Sol. *What good will come of this? How will this be fixed? All is lost.* But he kept running and running and running.

CHAPTER 13

the beginning

THE GRAVEL ROAD LEADING to the farmhouse was a mix of muddied earth and stones, Jeremy's sneakers deep in muck as he ran past the tractor. All was still, motionless as if abandoned, the pelting rain trying to cleanse the tractor of its memory, its metal frame voicing discontent with every raindrop. The weight of it had flattened the neatly furrowed garden, its bounty harvested, its soil barren.

Jeremy knocked on the door to no answer. He walked to the open window and peered in. Roy was sitting on the leather chair in the living room. Jeremy called out, but he didn't answer. Jeremy ran back to the front door and entered the farmhouse slinging a trail of mud and anguish.

"Roy. Roy. Roy!" Jeremy said. Nothing. He walked to the chair and gently tapped Roy's knee. He was too cold to the touch and his face was too pale. There was no breath and no life. Jeremy stepped backward, frightened, Roy gone and this stranger before him. His body tightened, air escaped his lungs, and he fell to his knees before the dead. He tried to scream but his vocal cords produced nothing. And then fear left him, replaced by an anguished cry.

"You promised!"

The cry of a selfish child.

A great rush of tears poured forth. They fell through Jeremy's anguished hands and onto Roy's shoes. They washed them clean. Clean of mud, clean of his last steps on this earth, and clean of the last few carcasses of empty melting caplets and liquid medicine stuck to them. Before Jeremy on the wooden floor, a floor shaped and formed from Roy's ancestors' hands from trees of this land, the Dead Sea, a pool of tears mixed with pharmaceuticals. It would evaporate, the only trace a stain and a memory. But for now it reflected Jeremy's strained face. He took a closer look. It was familiar yet different. The memory of the last year captured in the landscape of his face. Jeremy knew he must not be fueled by anger, even when the world constantly spits on you. *Make your own way and live the worthy life,* Roy told him. *One no medicine can provide. And spit back . . . when appropriate.* Tears broke his reflection, his suspicion confirmed—the graffiti in the nurse's office, the word *comportment* ricocheting in his heated brain. He now knew that Roy's last act on this earth was his last lesson, and as always it had ended not with math, not with physics, not with aerodynamics, not with meteorology, not with science. *And that is what good will come of this day.*

"I bet you were laughing, you old goat. You knew the security cameras were there. You didn't care, did you?" Jeremy said, a grin intruding on his sadness. "They won't listen but I will. What did you tell them? You should have seen the principal's face when the cop told him. You told them to fuck off, didn't you? The spray paint on the fridge and a wave good-bye—no, not a wave but a one-fingered salute, didn't you?"

Roy seemed to be smiling in death, and on his lap, he clutched his wedding photo. Faded sepia. Jeremy stared at the newlyweds sitting on a picnic blanket on a sunny summer day. The Stearman's wings provided shade, the sun warmth, and the farm sustenance as they began their life together.

"You did keep your promise. You did."

He remembered Roy's words: "But when you're up there, above it all looking down, you realize that you've become more connected with the world you're trying to free yourself from. The view is magnificent, the perspective even better."

It didn't ease the loss, but it lessened the pain. The screams of the selfish child were replaced by the maturity of the young man he had become. How he had wanted Roy to watch him move up from the Cub to the Stearman and to graduate from school. "What do I do now, Roy?" Jeremy stared at Roy, taking in death, the stillness, silence, and finality of it all. He rose to his feet, leaned over, and kissed Roy on the forehead.

"I don't know how, but I'll make you proud. Thank you for everything, Roy Higgins." Jeremy walked past the empty hospital bed, past the kitchen table, and out into the rain. Passing the open window, he took one last look at his friend, tears and raindrops falling onto the porch. Jeremy saluted the best he knew how.

Every drop of rain was a tap on the shoulder from the sky. A reminder from the man who taught him how to rise above the muck and shit of this world. Jeremy walked onto the open field. Welcoming sky and permitting earth. He extended his arms and leaned back, his face and chest greeting the rain. He knew that his shadow had left him, no Jesus on the cross, no Stearman standing on its tail. The scarecrow looked at Jeremy as if it were being replaced.

He's of earth. He's of sky. Never of one. A foot in both. Earth, sky, and Jeremy.

The father, the son, the holy spirit.

The American Harvester, the Cub, the Stearman.

His mom, Roy, Sarah.

The grass runway divided into thirds.

Beginning, middle, end.

He had to act or drown in the Dead Sea, but what to do. He heard the police sirens in the distance. He saw the flashing red and blue from the police cruisers moving across the gray sky. The earth permits and the heavens reveal. He looked at the withered ragged doll protecting the barren garden and the idle tractor beside the barn.

As Mellencamp, his mom's favorite singer, said, "There is rain on the scarecrow and blood on the plow."

He knew. It was time to go. But where to? He did not know and asked again and again. "Where?!" he asked at the top of his voice, the echo bouncing off the trees and returning with no answer. He remembered the foolish promise he made to himself in the school cafeteria a lifetime ago: *I'll take that plane and one day go to the ends of the earth.* Delusions of youth perhaps, but he wasn't that boy anymore. A dream fulfilled, and with that responsibility. But to whom? He wanted to stay now more than ever, but they were coming.

"She will find me! I know she will! She said so!"

Jeremy ran to the barn and opened the large doors. He pushed the Cub to the side and, with all his strength, pulled on the tow bar connected to the Stearman's landing gear. It resisted. The slumbering elephant didn't want to be taken from the warm comfort of the barn. It was familiar with the young boy but untrusting and would not budge. There was no time to argue—the sounds of sirens were near. He looked at the welcoming Cub. No! Jeremy ran outside and jumped on the tractor.

The diesel engine shook as he put it in gear, the smell of exhaust familiar, its growl comforting. The tractor's wheels rolled firmly over the muck and muddied earth as he drove toward the open barn. Jeremy positioned the harvester in front of the Stearman and slowly backed up. He connected the tow bar to the tractor and the Stearman relented, rolling into the open air of field and rain. The tow bar disconnected, Jeremy drove the tractor onto the gravel road, blocking the way to the farmhouse.

He ran back to the Stearman as the teachings of his mentor flooded through him. As if in dream he was outside himself, every movement effortless and confident. But this was no dream.

He jumped on the biplane's lower wing and, reaching over the top one, he opened the gas cap and saw that the tanks were full. The gas cap secure, he peered into the rear cockpit, confirming that the electrical switches were off before heading to the prop. He stopped. The metal plaque above the altimeter caught his attention: REAR SEAT FOR SOLO FLIGHT. The small circular mirror attached to the upper wing reflected the vacant rear cockpit. *Unless you know how to fly this thing I suggest the front one.* He stepped down off the wing and the mirror reflected his image. Rear seat for solo flight.

The silver ball floated around full, the fuel tanks were topped, and the eight gallons of oil, the color and consistency of silky gold, assured that the five-hundred-pound Lycoming engine would not rip itself apart. There was no time to sump the fuel for water, but Jeremy knew that the Stearman had been in the barn protected from the rains. The ailerons moved freely and the guy wires were taut, securing both wings. He removed the various covers and, after a quick inspection of the engine and cowl, hand-propped the engine. Seven turns of the prop and the Lycoming engine wheezed as it should. And for the first time Jeremy believed that, at least on this day, the bind of gravity and the weight of society would not ground him. He unfastened the safety clip next to the engine, drew the cylindrical metal syringe outward, away from the flush skin of the fuselage, primed the engine, and secured the syringe. The wheels had sufficient gum and enough air, the brakes had ample meat. A quick inspection of the rudder and elevator indicated that all was in order. The world would not drag him down. It was time.

Jeremy climbed into the rear cockpit. The view was different as he strapped into the shoulder harness and lap belt. He sat higher in the seat and farther back, his view expansive. It was a better view, a bigger view with a sense of being in charge. He was in charge but not in control. Sixteen-year-olds never are, only the dead are, the difference being the dead know. The sirens of the oncoming police cars went silent as he secured the leather skullcap and cinched the strap beneath his chin. He positioned the boom mike against his lips and pressed the intercom button. "One, two, three, four." He heard his voice in the headphones and no other. He pressed on the brakes, opened the throttle a half inch, and turned on the master electrical switch. "Clear prop!" Jeremy shouted as he looked toward the farmhouse, the scarecrow returning his gaze and no other.

Jeremy held his hand against the starter but didn't turn the switch. An unexpected sliver of sun broke through the steel-plate sky and a slice of youthful maturity entered his thoughts. *I'd be running away.* Self-doubt cut and confidence left him. The plane was airworthy, the weather clearing, but the pilot unsure, his decision now as uncertain as the forecasted weather. Only the dead and God know the forecast; the rest of us muddle through somehow. He dropped his hand away from the starter switch and sank into the seat, his shoulders sagged, and his chin fell to his chest. How do you ever know for certain that you're doing the right thing? He saw the FAA sectional chart sticking out from the navigation pouch, pulled it out, and read.

This is where I would go! The future is yours, Jeremy, and so is she. Take care of her. To the defiant, to the rebels, and to the journey. Take her west and see the country, and the world will open to you! You'll be fine. I promise. Your friend, Roy. The Old Goat.

He sat in silence, taking in the message.

"It's time. Here's to spitting back. Prop clear!" He turned the starter switch and the engine groaned and spat. It was a good spit, a purposeful spit, a surly spit. Jeremy drew the fumes into his lungs and tasted the smoke of the defiant, of the rebel, of the crucified, of Roy resurrected in him. The smoke dispersed and the shake of the engine became the mighty rhythmic beat of internal combustion. Roy's gifts to Jeremy were many, flight being one, but not the most important. He would not be alone. They were with him, Red, his mom, the members of the One of Us club, and Carol Morgan Spring. He doubted that the larger world would answer in kind, but he would trust his mentor and find out. He wouldn't be flying alone because Jeremy knew as Roy knew, as those he loved knew—We *are all broken, all fugitives in a world of broken fugitives.* He had to believe he was flying toward something and not away and that she would find him.

Jeremy taxied to the end of the farm, the slight branches at the oak treetops swaying in the breeze, the rusted metal weather vane atop the barn agreeing with the trees. He turned the nose of the Stearman toward the Great South Bay, the entire length of the farm before him. He stepped on the brakes; the flight controls were free and clear as he increased the throttles. The Stearman bucked, demanding to gallop as he checked the magnetos and confirmed that the carburetor heat was working properly. He cycled the propeller and set the trim for takeoff.

The engine back to idle, Jeremy took one last look, not at the Stearman but the farm. He looked toward the tail and saw a hole in the forest. Goggles drawn from his skullcap to his watering eyes, he grinned as he pushed the mixture control to full rich, the prop to full increase, and the throttle forward.

The Lycoming engine roared and the Stearman accelerated. Jeremy felt the weight of his life pressing him into his seat. The tail lifted, the control yoke centered, and the spray of rain droplets splattered on the wing disappeared. The balls of his feet pressed on the rudder, pedals keeping the galloping Stearman aligned with the fescue grass runway. His feet hurt from the day's events, but now it was a good hurt.

Fifty-five miles per hour. The wings took hold, the ground

relented, and the Stearman elevated into the sky. He rose. They rose and the rhythmic vibration of the Lycoming's engine resonated through his hands and body.

The Stearman flew past property's edge, its wake bending the trees as if they waved good-bye, the leaves atop the birch tree matching the yellow wings of the lone Cub in the barn. The crickets chirped and the birds sang as they dug for seedlings in the wet earth. And for the first time in 160 years there was no human to hear nature's symphony. The damp, cool breeze swirled across the farm and entered the open window of the farmhouse and chilled the decaying corpse. Nothing last forever except the earth and sky.

The familiar rhythmic vibration of the Stearman comforted Jeremy through his young hands. He had worked hard to understand the physics of flight and the laws of navigation, no longer magic and no longer dream, they and a full tank of gas his only willful constraints. Flying south, his castle by the sea passed underneath the Stearman, its shadow a brief but welcome guest among the catbrier and sand. The *Stranger* made its last outbound run of the day, its wake turning the greenish-blue water white as it departed the mainland. Passengers waved at the yellow flying machine and Jeremy tipped his wing. Before him was the Atlantic Ocean. He turned right following the shoreline of Fire Island. The steel gray sky had broken and a few more rays of sun cast their fingers upon the earth. Upon him. Jeremy tuned the radio and keyed the mike:

"New York Approach, Stearman November Five Three Two Niner Two, VFR request," Jeremy said.

"Stearman N53292, New York Approach, go ahead."

"Stearman N53292 is a Bravo 75, 500 feet, VFR one mile south of Robert Moses Bridge requesting transition through the Class B airspace, westbound."

"Roger. Squawk 4322," the controller said. Jeremy dialed the code into the transponder. "You are cleared into the Class B airspace. Where are you going?"

Where am I going?

He turned toward the open sea, unabated by man's indignities and trying to outrun man's scurrilous hands. And hoping, just hoping, that something good would come of this.

"West. I'm going west."